Emma fell against the door, thrown off balance by the speed of the turn. "Slow down," she snapped, fumbling for her seat belt.

"I can't." Sawyer ground the words out. He adjusted his white-knuckle grip on the steering wheel and pressed the limp brake pedal into the floorboards. "My brakes are out."

"What?" Her eyes widened.

Before them, a line of cars plugged away behind a slow-moving school bus on the road ahead of them. He jammed his thumb against his emergency flashers and continued a battering assault on his horn. His truck was out of control, and if the cars didn't move, he was going to take them all out with him.

Tiny horrified faces came into view, staring back at him through the dusty emergency exit.

Sawyer couldn't stop. Couldn't slow. Couldn't hit a busload of children at his current speed or they would all be dead, thrown over the mountain or fatally broken on impact.

With no other choice, Sawyer gritted his teeth and resolved to leave the road at any cost.

MISSING IN THE MOUNTAINS

JULIE ANNE LINDSEY

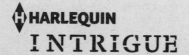

HARLEQUIN
INTRIGUE

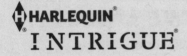

HARLEQUIN®
INTRIGUE®

Recycling programs
for this product may
not exist in your area.

ISBN-13: 978-1-335-13630-5

Missing in the Mountains

Copyright © 2020 by Julie Anne Lindsey

This edition published by arrangement with Harlequin Books S.A.

For questions and comments about the quality of this book,
please contact us at CustomerService@Harlequin.com.

Harlequin Enterprises ULC
22 Adelaide St. West, 40th Floor
Toronto, Ontario M5H 4E3, Canada
www.Harlequin.com

Printed in U.S.A.

Julie Anne Lindsey is an obsessive reader who was once torn between the love of her two favorite genres: toe-curling romance and chew-your-nails suspense. Now she gets to write both for Harlequin Intrigue. When she's not creating new worlds, Julie can be found carpooling her three kids around northeastern Ohio and plotting with her shamelessly enabling friends. Winner of the Daphne du Maurier Award for Excellence in Mystery/Suspense, Julie is a member of International Thriller Writers, Romance Writers of America and Sisters in Crime. Learn more about Julie and her books at julieannelindsey.com.

Books by Julie Anne Lindsey

Harlequin Intrigue

Fortress Defense

Deadly Cover-Up
Missing in the Mountains

Garrett Valor

Shadow Point Deputy
Marked by the Marshal

Protectors of Cade County

Federal Agent Under Fire
The Sheriff's Secret

Visit the Author Profile page at Harlequin.com.

CAST OF CHARACTERS

Emma Hart—Steadfast single mother and recent witness to the abduction of her older sister, Sara. Emma reaches out to a private security firm for help but never expects the man who fathered her child and then broke her heart will be the one who shows up at her door.

Sawyer Lance—Recently discharged army ranger and current cofounder of Fortress Security, a private security firm created to protect civilians in danger. Sawyer's been stateside less than a month when a familiar voice calls for help. Now he'll stop at nothing to protect the woman he's always loved and the baby he never knew he had.

Henry Lance—The four-month-old son of Emma and Sawyer.

Sara Hart—Older sister of Emma Hart and local credit union account specialist. Sara's been keeping a secret from Emma, and now she's been brutally attacked and abducted.

Christopher Lawson—The diligent credit union IT staffer who fielded Sara's calls on an issue she shouldn't have had.

Detective Rosen—Local detective assigned to the disappearance of Sara Hart.

Detective Miller—Local detective willing to work with Sawyer to bring Sara home.

Chapter One

Emma Hart couldn't shake the unsettling notion that something was wrong. The sensation had pestered her all day, needling away at her calm. Though she hadn't said so, her sister and housemate, Sara, seemed to feel it too. Sara had hunched over her cell phone and a notebook most of the day, barely speaking or touching her dinner. It wasn't like Sara to be inside short of a blizzard, yet there she was. All day.

Emma had thrown herself into the tedium of housework and the exhaustion of new-mommy duties, hoping to keep her mind off the inexplicable feeling that trouble was afoot. Nothing had worked. The prickle over her skin that had raised the hair on her arms and itched in her mind since dawn refused to let up, even now as the gorgeous setting sun nestled low on the horizon between distant mountains. If there was a silver lining, it was that the peculiar day was finally nearing its end, and tomorrow was always better.

She crossed her ankles on the old back-porch

swing and shifted her attention to the beautiful gold and apricot hues spilling over everything in sight, including her perfect baby boy, Henry. Emma hoisted him off her lap and wiggled him in the air until a wide toothless grin emerged. There was the thing she lived for. A smile spread over her lips as she brought him down to her chest. "Someday I'm going to teach you to rope and ride, the way your granddaddy taught Sara and me." It would have been nice if Henry's father was around to teach him those things the way her father had taught her, but it didn't do to dwell on what wasn't, not when the things that were tended to be so fleeting.

Henry's daddy was a soldier on leave when they'd met, but he'd been raised a cowboy. Brought up on a ranch like hers, not too far from there, but he'd been deployed before she'd known she was pregnant, and despite the voice message she'd left asking him to call her, he never had. Of course, that wasn't a surprise since the next time she'd tried to call him the number was no longer in service. The local news hadn't announced his death the way they often did when a local soldier was lost, so she could only assume he'd survived that "eight week" mission he'd gone on nearly a year ago and had simply chosen to avoid her after his return. Whenever she thought of how his selfishness would force Henry to grow up without a father, Emma was glad he hadn't died on that mission. This way, if she ever saw him again, she could kill him herself.

Emma forced down the bitter knot rising in her throat and worked a pleasant smile over her lips. "You will always be enough for me," she promised Henry, "and I will be enough for you. Whatever that means on any given day. Always." She nuzzled his sun-kissed cheek, then stretched onto her feet as the last orange fingers of the sunlight slid out of view, replaced with the tranquil blues of twilight. "What do you say about a warm bath and fuzzy jammies before your nighttime bottle?" she asked. Now she needed a distraction from the icky feeling that had followed her all day *and* from the frustration of a man who'd probably forgotten her name.

Emma jumped as the back door flew open, her knuckles colliding sharply with the handle. "What on earth!"

Sara stood on the threshold, one palm on the door, skin pale as the rising moon. "You need to come inside. Now," she gasped. "Hurry."

Emma obeyed, and Sara locked the door behind them, then checked the window locks and pulled the curtains. Without speaking again, she moved to the next room and did the same.

"What's going on?" Emma followed on her sister's heels, fear riding high in her gut. "Why are you doing that?" They only battened down the hatches if the news predicted heavy winds or rain. "It's a beautiful night. There's no storm coming."

"You're wrong about that," Sara mumbled.

Emma hurried around her sister, forcing herself into Sara's path. "Hey. What's that supposed to mean?"

Sara shot her a remorseful look, letting her gaze slide briefly to Henry, then back to her work. "I need you to listen to me and do as I say. We have to be quiet." Her hands trembled as she reached for the nearest light switch and flipped it off. Her face whipped back in Emma's direction a moment later. "Is your truck in the garage? Or the driveway?"

"Garage."

"Good." She nodded, her eyes frantic.

"Hey." Emma set her hand on Sara's. "Stop." Her sister never behaved this way. She was naturally calm to the extreme, cool in a crisis and found the positive in everything. Whatever had her so worked up was enough to make Emma want to pack a bag and move. "You're scaring me. Tell me what's going on."

Fat tears welled in Sara's eyes. "I can't."

"Sara," Emma demanded, using her most pointed tone without upsetting Henry, "you can tell me anything. You know that. I don't understand what's happened. You were fine at dinner."

Sara snorted, a derisive, ugly sound. "Was I?"

"Weren't you?" Emma grabbed hold of her sister's wrist, a lifelong stubborn streak piercing her forced calm.

Before she could answer, a set of headlights flashed over the front window, and Sara froze. "Don't make any noise," she said, looking half-ill. "We're not home."

Suddenly Sara's erratic behavior began making sense. "Is this the reason you're locking us up like Fort Knox?" Emma asked. "You knew someone was coming?" Someone who obviously terrified her. "Who?"

Sara jerked her arm free and went to peek through the living room curtain. "Hide," she seethed. "You're in danger. Henry's in danger. We all are. Now, go! Keep him quiet. Find his pacifier." Her rasping whisper cut through Emma's heart, and she pressed her back to the nearest wall, away from the front window.

"Not until you tell me what's going on," Emma shot back in a harsh whisper.

Heavy footfalls rumbled across the porch, and someone rapped against the door in loud, demanding strikes until Emma was sure the door would fall down.

"I'm calling the police," Emma said. "If you won't tell me what's going on, then you can tell them."

Henry started in her arms. He released a small whimper as the pounding continued.

Sara turned to them. Her eyes were wide, her face the perfect mask of horror and resolve. "Hide first. Call the police after." She rubbed her palms against her jeans and stepped forward, toward the rattling door.

"Where are you going?"

Sara gave Emma a pleading look, then swallowed hard. "I'm going to answer the door before he breaks it down. If you hide, he'll assume I'm alone, and you'll be safe, but I won't give him what he wants."

Emma's stomach twisted and coiled with nausea. "What does he want?"

Sara took another step.

"I won't leave you."

Sara shot one determined glance over her shoulder. "Your job is to protect Henry. Mine is to protect you. Now, hide."

Terror gripped Emma, and she snagged the cordless phone handset from the wall, immediately dialing the local police department. She ducked around the edge of the living room wall, hiding just out of sight in the long hallway that led to the bedrooms. "Come on," she urged, impatient for the ringing call to connect.

The dead bolt snicked back in the next room. The door swung open on squeaky hinges.

"I've already called the police," Sara said coldly in lieu of a proper greeting.

A choking gasp cracked through the silence a moment later.

Emma sucked air. Horrific images of what could have caused such a sound raced through her head. There were no more words in the silent home. Just the low gurgling of someone desperate for air. Emma prayed the sound wasn't coming from Sara.

A tinny voice broke through the phone speaker at her ear. "Knox Ridge Police Department."

Emma inched toward the end of the hall, ignoring

the woman on the line. Desperate to know her sister was okay, she counted silently to three, then peeked her head around the corner, chest tight with fear.

A man in head-to-toe black, a ski mask and leather gloves had one giant hand wrapped around Sara's throat while she clawed uselessly at his fingers. Her eyes were wild, bulging, her mouth gaping for air. The man raised a pistol in his free hand.

Hot tears rushed over Emma's eyes. She had the police on the phone, but couldn't speak. If the man heard her, he might use his gun on Sara. *Or on Henry.*

Hide. Sara's desperate voice echoed in Emma's addled mind. *Protect Henry.*

"Knox Ridge Police Department," the woman on the phone repeated. Her small voice suddenly sounded like a booming gong.

Henry bunched his face and opened his quivering lips, a scream poised to break.

Emma took one last too-risky look into the living room, needing assurance her sister hadn't been choked to death while she'd stood helplessly by and deliberated over what to do next.

The man tossed Sara onto the couch like a rag doll and climbed on top of her in a flash. He lowered his face to hers and growled through the mask. "Who did you tell?" He pinned her hands overhead and pressed them hard into the cushions until they vanished from sight.

"No one." Sara choked out the words, still coughing and gasping for air. "No one. I have no one to tell. I swear it."

Henry released a warning cry, and the man's face snapped in Emma's direction.

Emma rocked back on socked feet and took off like a bullet down the hallway. Henry bounced and jostled in her arms as she pressed him to her chest and gripped the phone between one ear and shoulder. She slid and scooted as adrenaline forced her legs faster than her feet could find purchase on the hard, slick floors.

"What was that?" the man asked, footsteps already falling through the living room, nearing the hall at a clip.

"Cat!" Sara yelped. "It was only the cat."

Emma snatched their mean old barn cat off the hallway windowsill on her way to the master bedroom, and she threw him into the space behind her. He'd surely bite her the next time he saw her, but she'd gladly choose to face off with him rather than whoever was attempting to murder Sara.

The cat screeched and hissed, claws skidding over the wide wooden planks as he slid in the direction of Sara and the masked lunatic.

The footfalls stopped.

Emma barreled into her closet and pulled the door shut behind her. Her heart hammered and her chest ached. She climbed through the clothes racks, over boxes and blankets and shoes, then curled herself around her son and shushed him out of a fast-approaching fit.

Several wild heartbeats later, the footfalls retreated back toward her sister, who she hoped had had the good sense to run.

"Who did you tell?" the man's voice came again, impossibly angrier.

Emma's heart fell. Sara hadn't run.

"Ma'am?" the voice asked through the phone. "Miss Hart? Caller ID shows this as the Hart residence?"

What was happening? *Why* was it happening?

"Miss Hart," the woman persisted.

"Yes," she whispered, finally finding her voice. She cringed with each terrorizing demand of the intruder in the next room. *Who did you tell?*

Sara screamed.

Her gut-wrenching wail ripped through the rafters, the drywall and Emma's soul. "Someone is hurting my sister," she whispered. "Please, hurry."

Emma's gaze darted through the dark space. If only she hadn't moved her daddy's rifles into a gun safe after Henry was born. If only Henry was sleeping in his crib, and she could trust him not to scream. If only she could help Sara.

A deafening crack stopped her ragged thoughts. The sound of skin on skin. A brain-jarring slap. Or jaw-breaking punch. Every sound was amplified in the impossibly still home. Emma heard the muted thud of a collapsing body.

Then no more screaming. No more demanding growls. Just silence.

Outside, the rumble of an engine drew hope to Emma's heart. The psychopath was leaving. Whatever condition Sara was in, at least she hadn't been shot, and the police were on the way. Sara would be okay, and she would tell them everything so the son of a gun who did this to her would pay.

Emma crept from her hiding spot and raced to her bedroom window, confirming the empty driveway before racing back down the hallway, heart in her throat and preparing to provide triage while they awaited the first responders.

On a deep intake of air, she shored her nerve at the end of the hallway, tucked Henry tight to her chest and dared a peek into her living room.

But all that remained of her sister was a thick smear of blood on the polished wooden floor.

Chapter Two

Sawyer Lance, former Army Ranger and cofounder of Fortress Security, reached reluctantly for the ringing phone. It was late and he was tired. Protecting civilians was harder than he'd predicted when opening the private sector security firm. Far more challenging than similar work overseas where he could at least shoot the bad guys. He tossed another pair of aspirin into his mouth before blindly raising the phone from his desk.

What would it be this time? Another punk ex-husband or boyfriend bullying the woman he claimed to love? An unhinged stranger stalking a woman who didn't know he existed beyond the fact he harassed her anonymously with creepy unwanted gifts and the occasional break-in? "Fortress," he answered, his voice little better than a bark. "This is Sawyer Lance."

The long pause that followed was nearly cause for him to hang up. Instead, he rubbed his forehead, knowing sometimes frightened folks needed time to gather their thoughts.

"Fortress," he repeated, becoming alert at the sound of soft breaths through the line. His muscles tensed. "If this is an emergency, you need to call 911 and get yourself to safety. Call me after. Police first."

He waited.

The quiet breathing continued.

"I can contact your local authorities if you're unable." Sawyer pulled the phone away from his ear and checked the caller ID. "Can you tell me your..." Two little words graced the screen and nearly ripped a hole through his chest. *Emma. Hart.* Sawyer's heart seized, and his lungs seemed to stop midexhale. "Emma?"

Emma Hart had been the only woman Sawyer ever imagined a future with, and a set of monsters overseas had stolen that from him. He'd been forced to say goodbye to her for the sake of a simple eight-week mission. That mission should have brought him right up to his last day in the service. Instead, it had gotten him captured and tortured. His team had gotten worse.

"You're alive," she said, a snare of accusation in her voice.

"Yeah." If she wanted to call it that. He'd fought six long months to get away from his captors and back to the secluded US military base. Another two months before he was debriefed and returned stateside. More weeks before the long-overdue discharge.

"Yet, you never called," she said.

Emma's message had been the last one left on his cell phone before the service was disconnected.

The cell contract had ended while he was overseas, trapped for months past the contract's renewal date. He'd planned to get a new phone after the mission, after he'd returned stateside and been discharged. He'd even told himself Emma's number would be the first one he'd call. It was one of many plans his captivity had ruined.

"No," he answered finally, sadly.

He hadn't returned her call for multiple reasons. Part of him knew he wasn't ready to do normal things again, like date, or pretend he didn't wake up in cold sweats most nights. The rest of him doubted Emma was in the market for a 180-pound sack of misplaced anger, jangled nerves and general distrust. He couldn't make her happy anymore. *She'd sounded so darn happy on that voice mail.* Unlike now, he realized.

Instinct stiffened Sawyer's spine. "What's wrong?" Something in her voice set him on edge. She might've been mad at him, but there was something else there too.

"Sara's gone," she said, her voice breaking on the second word.

"Gone?" he repeated. His mind scrambled to make sense of the word. "How? When?"

"Tonight," she said. "He just came in here and took her."

Sawyer was already on his feet, gathering his things, shoving a fresh magazine into his sidearm. "Who?"

"I don't know. She told me to hide."

He slowed, pressing a folding knife and wallet into his pocket. "So, Sara's alive? Just missing?"

"I don't know if she's alive," Emma snapped, "but she's not *just missing*. She was choked, overpowered, hit and dragged away. There's nothing *just* about it."

"Of course." Sawyer shook his head hard, moving faster toward the exit. "I meant no disrespect. I'm only gathering facts." He stooped to grab his go-bag and a duffel of supplies from the closet floor. "What did the police say?"

"They're looking into it."

Sawyer blew out a humorless half laugh. So, the police were chasing their tails and waiting for Sara to appear on their laps. "I'm glad you called. I can keep you safe." He swung his laptop bag over one shoulder on his way out the door.

"You always talked about your plans to open Fortress Security with Wyatt," Emma said. "I figured he'd answer the call. I hoped he'd remember me and be willing to help. I didn't know what else to do."

"You did the right thing," he assured her.

"I know the last thing you probably want to do is see me—" her voice was strangled and tight "—but I'm scared, and I need help."

"I'm already on the way," Sawyer said, tossing his bags into his pickup, then climbing behind the wheel. "Are you home?"

"Yeah."

He gunned the engine to life and jammed the

shifter into Drive. "I'm heading your way from the office. I won't be an hour."

"Okay."

He listened keenly to a few more rattling breaths. "Sawyer?"

The quaver in her voice was a punch through his gut. "Yeah."

"You should have called."

EMMA'S WORDS HAUNTED him as he made the trip to her family ranch at a record pace, nearly doubling the posted speed limits whenever possible. The desolate country roads were poorly lit but easily navigated. At times, long stretches between darkened fields made visibility clear for miles, and Sawyer took full advantage. The hillier, curvier portions got a good cussing.

He hit the gravel under the carved Hart Ranch sign with a deep crunch and grind. Stones pinged and bounced against the undercarriage of his pickup, flying out in a cloud of dust behind him.

A small silhouette paced the porch. Long hair drifting in the wind around her face, exactly like the ghost from his past that she was. She went still when he started his walk across the lawn.

Sawyer pulled the cowboy hat off his head and pressed it to his aching chest. "Emma." His lungs seemed to fill fully for the first time since answering her call.

She gave a small nod, running the pads of both

thumbs beneath red puffy eyes and brushing shaky palms over flushed cheeks. "Hello, Sawyer."

He took a step closer, and she wrapped her arms around a new, curvier figure. Sawyer tried not to stare, but the change looked damn good on her. So did the spark of ferocity in her eyes. He didn't know what had sparked the fire, but whatever it was, the change suited her. And it would help her get through the tough days ahead. Unfortunately, civilian abductions weren't known for their happy endings.

She appraised him as he climbed the steps. Her smart blue eyes scrutinized the visible scars along his neck and forearms, pausing briefly at the angry, puckered skin above his left eye. Then swiftly moving on to the lines of black ink circling his biceps beneath one shirtsleeve. "Thank you for coming."

"Of course."

Behind her, the small sound of a crying baby drifted through the open door.

Emma's chin ticked up. She turned immediately. "Come in. I've been through all of Sara's things, and I have something I want you to look at."

Sawyer followed. His heart clenched as the baby's cries grew more fervent. "Sara had a baby?" He tried to imagine it and failed. The willowy blonde had more interest in horses than men when he'd briefly known her.

"No." Emma grabbed the flashing baby monitor and shut it off as she passed through the dimly lit family room. "You can have a seat. I'll only be a minute."

"Are you babysitting?" he asked, ignoring her order and following her down the hall toward the bedrooms, unwilling to let her out of his sight and drawn by a strange tether to the infant's cry. "Was the baby here when Sara was taken?"

Emma opened her bedroom door and strode inside. A crib stood against the wall across from her bed. "No," she said, "and yes."

Sawyer paused at the end of the crib, puzzling over her unnecessary coyness. "You aren't babysitting?" he asked dumbly, watching as she raised the kicking blue bundle into her arms and slid a pacifier into the baby's mouth with practiced skill.

"No," she whispered, rocking the infant gently into sedation. "This is Henry." She turned a pride-filled smile in Sawyer's direction. "I named him after my father."

Sawyer's gut rolled against his spine. His jaw locked, and his fingers curled into fists at his sides. This was what had changed her. The carefree woman he'd known had been made into her own kind of soldier in his absence. Emma was a mother. "He's yours," Sawyer said, repeating the fact, trying to make it real for him. The words were bittersweet on his tongue. Any joy he might've felt for her was tainted selfishly with feelings of loss for himself. With regret. And thoughts of things that might have been. "You have a son."

"I do," she answered as Henry worked the pacifier in his tiny mouth. "And so do you."

EMMA HELD HER tongue as she waited for a response. She could practically see the wheels turning in Sawyer's head, adding up time, weeks, months. She ground her teeth against the need for an explanation. She hadn't been with anyone else since Sawyer. He'd barely left the States before she knew she was pregnant. If Henry's perfect olive skin and pale blue eyes weren't enough proof, then maybe Sawyer should look in a mirror.

"Mine?" His gaze jumped continually between her face and Henry's.

"Yes." She moved past him toward the hallway. "I need to sit down. You probably should too."

She led Sawyer back into the living room, giving a wide berth to the freshly bleached floorboards where Sara's blood had been spilled. She took a seat on the chair farthest from the couch where the monster had pinned her sister. It took effort to force the still-raw images from her mind.

Sawyer squatted on the floor in front of her chair, jeans pulled tight against his strong thighs, big hands dangling between his knees as he balanced, a look of shock and confusion etched on his brow. "Why didn't you tell me?"

Emma pursed her lips, culling the desire to scream. "I tried." She made each word stand on its own, tempted to recite all the one-sided arguments she'd practiced to perfection in the shower all these months since his "eight week" mission ended.

"I got a message from you," he said. "Did you know you were pregnant when you left the voice mail?"

The accusation in his tone ignited a fire in her belly. "That was why I called. I'd just confirmed with my doctor, and I was happy," she snapped.

"Then why didn't you tell me? Why would you keep something like this from me? I'm a father, Emma. A *father* and I had no idea."

"You could have returned my call," she said.

"You could've told me in the voice mail."

"I didn't want to tell you something this important in a voice mail. I wanted to tell you in person, and you were supposed to be home in two more weeks, and I spent every one of those last fourteen days deciding how I'd deliver the surprise. Maybe with some cutesy sign or a little custom-made onesie." She shook her head. "I can see it was stupid of me now, but I was *thrilled* to be having your baby, and you had your phone number changed."

"I didn't have my number changed." Sawyer ground the words through clenched teeth.

"Disconnected then," she conceded, "without the courtesy of letting me know first. You made it clear you didn't want to hear from me again, and you didn't want to call me either, or you would have."

"That isn't what happened."

Emma squinted her eyes, wishing she could scream and yell and lose control, but she refused to frighten Henry or give Sawyer the satisfaction of see-ing her so rattled. Instead, she said, "I called your number every month after my prenatal appointment, and I listened to the notification that your number had been disconnected. I forced myself to remember you were done with me, even if my heart wasn't done with you, and you have no idea what that was like for me."

His frustrated expression fell slowly into a gri-mace. "I wasn't home when you left that voice mail. I didn't even get it until last month."

"Then you should have called last month."

"How could I have known this?" he asked, ex-tending a hand toward the baby in her arms. "It's been more than a year since we've spoken. I assumed you'd moved on."

Her eyebrows shot up. "I did. I'm fine. We're fine," she said, casting a gaze at her son. "I had to get my act together, with or without you, and I had to find peace for Henry's sake. So I stopped calling you, and I let us go."

He fixed a heated gaze on her, his face wrought with emotion. Hurt, frustration, regret. "What would've happened if Sara hadn't been taken today?" he asked. "I would've just gone on with my life hav-ing no idea I was a father?"

Emma glared back, wind sucked from her chest. She wanted to shove him hard and knock him onto his backside, but there wasn't time for that. "We can fight about this later. Right now I need to figure out what happened to Sara," she said. "I found a notebook full of numbers hidden in her room. Will you look at it for me and see if it makes any sense to you?"

"How old is he?" Sawyer asked, unmoved by her change of subject. His gaze was locked on Henry. "When was he born? What did he weigh?"

Emma steadied her nerves and wet her lips. Those were fair enough questions. "His name is Henry Sawyer Hart. He's four months old, born June 8 at 8:17 a.m. He weighed eight pounds, eleven ounces. He was twenty-one inches long."

"You gave him my name."

"Middle name. It seemed like the right thing to do."

Sawyer pressed the heels of his hands to his eyes and dug them in.

"Why didn't you call?" she asked again, needing to know once and for all what had happened between their last passionate night of love declarations and the dead silence that began afterward and never ended.

Sawyer dropped his hands from his eyes. He stretched onto his feet and braced broad hands over narrow hips. Warning flared in his eyes. There was a debate going on in that head of his, but his lips were sealed tight.

Maybe he didn't have a reason. Maybe he didn't want to admit their time together had been nothing more than a fling. Not real to him like it had been to her. It was easy to see he wasn't the same guy she'd fallen in love with. The man before her was hard and distant. Not the man who'd swept her into his arms and twirled her until she was breathless with laughter.

Maybe that guy had never been real.

Emma's throat tightened as the look on his face grew pained. "Never mind. You don't owe me an explanation." She lifted Sara's notebook from the end table beside her and extended it to Sawyer. "Here. Let's just move on. Maybe there's something in there that will help the police figure out who took her and why. She's been gone twenty-four hours already, and our odds of finding her diminish significantly after seventy-two."

Sawyer caught the narrow book in his fingertips and held her gaze. "My team and I were captured. They were killed."

Emma's mouth fell open. "What?"

"They died. I didn't. I've only been home a few weeks. My cell service plan wasn't renewed on time because I wasn't home, so it was canceled. I didn't change the number or disconnect the phone. I wasn't thinking about any of that. I was trying to survive, and I don't want to talk about what happened."

She worked her mouth shut. Her own harsh words crashed back to mind like a ton of bricks. She'd blamed him for not returning her calls without bothering to ask why he hadn't. She'd assumed the worst, that he'd avoided her intentionally, played her for a fool, never realizing that him avoiding her was hardly the worst thing that could have happened. Her gaze snapped back to the scars. Thick, raised marks across his skin that weren't there a year ago. On his neck and arms. What looked like the results of a serious burn above his left eye. "Sawyer."

He lifted a palm. "Don't."

Emma cradled Henry tighter, comforting the one piece of Sawyer that would allow it. She'd heard stories, saw movies and read books about men who'd been through similar things, losing their teams, being held against their wills. There was a common thread to every man's story. Their experiences had wrecked them.

"I know what your sister is going through," Sawyer said, "not the physical details, but emotionally. Mentally." His serious blue eyes rose to meet her gaze. "I'll help find her," he said. "And I will keep you and Henry safe while I do."

Emma nodded. "Thank you."

He carried the notebook to the couch where Sara had fought with her attacker, and collapsed onto the cushions. He spread the notebook open across his palms, but his gaze continually moved to Emma's before sliding back to Henry.

"What?" Emma finally asked, her heart warming and softening toward the man she'd thought had tossed her away.

His eyes flashed dark and protective, but he didn't look away from his son. "You should've left that message."

Chapter Three

Sawyer didn't sleep. Emma had taken the barely manageable wreckage of his life and flipped it on its head. She might as well have flipped *him* on his head. He was a father.

The words had circled endlessly in his mind as he pored over the contents of Sara's notebook and made multiple trips down the hallway to check on Emma and Henry. *His son.*

A son he hadn't even known existed until a few hours ago. He might've never known about Henry at all if something horrible hadn't happened to Sara, forcing Emma to reach out for help. And Henry could've grown up thinking his father was the kind of man who would run out on a woman and his son.

It made him madder every time he thought about it.

He'd nearly missed the most important part of his life because pride had stopped him from returning Emma's call. And it sure wouldn't have killed her to add the life-changing detail to her message.

The glow of a pending sunrise hovered on the horizon when he finally put Sara's notebook on the kitchen table and went to make coffee. Down the hall, he heard the stirring sounds of Emma and his baby. Sawyer set the coffee to brew, then opened the refrigerator. By the time Emma and Henry emerged from their shared room, Sawyer had a simple breakfast prepared for two. "I hope you don't mind," he said. "Restless hands."

Emma stopped at the kitchen's edge, Henry on one hip. She'd dressed in nice-fitting blue jeans and a long-sleeved thermal shirt that hugged all her new curves in the nicest of ways. Her straight brown hair hung over her shoulders and feathered across her forehead.

Sawyer longed to run his fingers through the strands and pull her against him. He wanted to comfort her. To make promises for Sara's safety that he couldn't keep. He'd promised to find her, but if he didn't do that fast… His mind wandered to images of his fallen team.

"You didn't sleep," Emma said, fastening Henry into a high chair.

"Rarely do." He lifted a pan full of eggs from the stove and flicked the burner off, forcing his thoughts back to the present. "Hungry?"

"I don't know." She went to the counter to make a bottle for Henry. A moment later she took the seat beside the high chair and poised the bottle to Henry's lips. "I feel like none of this is real. Like I'm waiting to wake up from a nightmare."

Sawyer cleared his throat. "You should try to put a little something in your stomach."

Henry sucked greedily on the bottle, peering at Sawyer with big blue eyes. His denim overalls had little horses embroidered on the knees, and his tiny brown socks were printed to look like cowboy boots.

Sawyer's hands itched to hold him, but he divided the eggs onto two plates instead, then poured twin cups of coffee for Emma and himself. The idea of holding something as precious as Henry frightened him, and Sawyer was rarely afraid. He took a seat beside Emma at the table and wrapped calloused palms around the small white mug. His hands had done awful things in the name of freedom. His hands were meant for hard labor, for holding rifles and following orders.

Emma took a slice of plain toast from the pile he'd plated and set between them, and bit into the corner. "What did you think of Sara's notebook? It was hidden so it must be important, right?"

"Maybe." Sawyer dug a fork into his breakfast. "Sara works at a bank, right?"

"Credit union," Emma said. "She's an account specialist, and she had that notebook with her all day before she was taken. I found it hidden in a basket of dirty clothes. She must've put it there when she realized that man was coming for her."

Sawyer cleaned his plate and grabbed a second slice of toast. "I want to visit her office today. I wasted a ton of time overlooking the obvious. I was looking at the numbers like a soldier. Trying to solve them like a cipher. First, I assumed they were a code.

When that didn't work, I imagined them as dates and times or map coordinates, addresses, you name it." He gave a humorless chuckle. "Eventually I remembered Sara works at the credit union. Those numbers are probably a list of accounts. She's just jammed them all together, probably to disguise them."

Emma finished her toast and took away the empty baby bottle. "What are you going to do at the credit union?"

"I want to find out if she was working on any special projects. If any accounts or customers might've been giving her trouble, and if she seemed like herself the last few times she was in. I'd also really like to get a look at her desk. See if she kept any more notebooks like that one." He tipped his head toward the book on the table.

Emma unbuckled Henry from the high chair. "The police will probably be asking the same things today. The staff will be leery and guarded after that. Everyone loves Sara, and they don't know you. I doubt anyone will be candid with a stranger given what's happened." She turned Henry against her chest and patted his back. "I'll go. They know me. I'll ask to see her desk and try to collect anything that might be of interest. Then we can go through it here in privacy. If we find anything that leads to more specific questions, we can go back after lunch and ask."

Sawyer frowned. "I think you'd better let me be the face of this for you. As it is, whoever took Sara doesn't seem interested in you, and I'd rather you not get involved. Her abductor didn't even search the house while he was here. His mission was pointed. Not at you, and I'd like to keep it that way."

Emma chewed her lip, cheeks flushed with distress. "I'm Sara's only sister and I live with her. How long do you really think it will take before he comes for me? For Henry? If she doesn't give up whatever it is that he wants from her?"

Sawyer locked his jaw. The abductor would be smart to use Sara's family as leverage if she gave him any trouble. Sawyer's captors had tried the same thing. Eliminating his men one by one, using their allegiances to one another to find the weakest link. But there had been no weak link, and they had died. One by one. "All the more reason for you to stay out of sight."

"But if Sara was keeping a secret book of account numbers," Emma said, "then someone at the credit union might know something about her kidnapping, and I don't want to draw any attention that will keep me from getting a look at her desk. You—" she lifted a narrow finger at him "—draw attention."

Sawyer sucked his teeth. It wasn't the first time he'd heard it. His six-foot-two-inch frame had been thickened, hardened and cultivated during his time in the service. The added scars and tattoos only served to enhance his dangerous appearance. Slowly, he relaxed against the seat back. He didn't like it, but she had a point, and while he would have preferred to go in and throw some weight around, Emma's idea wasn't a bad one.

EMMA CLIMBED ONTO the curb across the street from the credit union, Henry on one hip, his empty diaper bag on her shoulder. "I won't be long," she told Sawyer, who made no pretense of agreeing with her decision to go in alone.

She shut the door and hurried along the crosswalk before the light changed. Traffic was tight on the normally quiet streets of downtown Knox Ridge. The sidewalks teemed with people enjoying a beautiful Saturday morning. The weekly farmers market was set up a few blocks away, and barricades closed the street to traffic at the next intersection, making parking a nightmare. They'd gotten lucky finding a space in view of the credit union, but it was just another thing Sawyer had complained about. He'd wanted to be closer. Preferably right in front of the door. As if Emma was somehow in danger on a busy sidewalk at ten in the morning.

An exiting customer saw Emma coming and held the door.

"Thank you," she said, slipping inside.

The credit union's interior was quiet. A line of people stood between rows of velvet ropes, awaiting their turn with a teller. The air smelled vaguely of aged paper and new carpet. And despite the fact it was barely October, instrumental holiday music drifted softly overhead.

Emma scanned the room for a familiar face that wasn't already with a customer.

Kate, the assistant manager, came swiftly into view. Her eyes widened when she caught sight of Emma, and she cut through the space in a flash. "Oh my goodness. How are you?" she asked. "The police were here this morning. They told me what happened. I can't believe it."

Emma swallowed a painful lump in her throat. She hadn't expected to get emotional at the mere mention of *what happened*. She'd had a hold on herself at home, but out in the world, knowing other people knew made Sara's abduction seem impossibly more real. "What did the police say?" Emma asked. "Do they have a suspect? Or a clue?" If so, no one had bothered to call Emma with the information.

"No. They were asking a lot of questions. None I could answer. I just saw Sara a few days ago and she was fine. She looked tired, maybe distracted, but not enough that I even thought to ask her about it. I mean, we're all tired, right?"

Emma certainly was. She took a breath and prepared her practiced line to get into Sara's desk. "Did the police go through her things? Would you mind if I did? I think she has the spare house key," Emma lied, "and now I'm paranoid someone will come walking in at night while I'm sleeping."

Kate paled. "Oh no. Of course. This way." She walked Emma to a row of cubicles along the far wall and waved an arm toward Sara's desk. "There it is. Take a look. I wouldn't know where to start."

Emma gave Kate her most pitiful face as she lowered onto her sister's chair. "Sara did seem tired. I'd assumed it was work-related stress. She probably had a lot on her plate or an extra difficult account."

Kate puzzled. "We're all overworked, but she never mentioned a difficult account. She had about a metric ton of questions a few weeks back on how our banking system works, but I had no clue. I directed her to Mr. Harrison." She pointed to an open office door across the room. A bearded, middle-aged guy was on the phone and already watching them from his desk, brow furrowed.

"Do you want to talk to him?" Kate asked. "He can tell you more about whatever Sara was doing." Her bottom lip poked out. "You must be trying to get your mind around her last few days."

"They weren't her last days," Emma snapped, surprising herself with the force of her words.

Kate started. "I didn't mean that," she said. "Not like that."

Emma stared, biting her lip and collecting her calm. "Sorry. I'm on edge. You understand." She flicked her gaze to Mr. Harrison, a normally kind man who looked suddenly agitated inside his office. "I don't think I'm ready to talk to anyone else." It might've been her restless night, her emotional state or sheer paranoia, but the branch manager seemed to have fixed his angry eyes on her, despite the line of patrons moving between them. If Mr. Harrison had anything to do with what had happened to Sara, then Emma wasn't in a hurry to run in there and ask about it. Better to let the police or Sawyer do that.

She lowered her eyes to the tidy piles on Sara's desk. "Did the police go through her things?"

"They looked," Kate said, "but they didn't take anything. They were more interested in how she'd been acting lately or if anyone had come to see her here that potentially upset her. Angry ex-boyfriends, things like that."

Right, Emma thought, *because the police didn't have the notebook.* She'd only located it last night while waiting for Sawyer to arrive. The police didn't have a reason to wonder if someone at her work was involved when they'd visited. Maybe Emma didn't either. Maybe the notebook was something else completely, and Emma was reaching for threads, for some way to feel more useful, when in truth there was nothing to do but wait.

She'd get the notebook to the detective in charge as soon as possible. Let him take it from here.

A door slammed and Emma gasped. She and Kate swung in the direction of the sound.

Mr. Harrison's door was closed.

"Kate?" A teller waved from across the room.

Kate frowned. "Sorry. I'll only be a minute," she told Emma.

"I'll be fine." A minute was all Emma needed. She swiveled on her sister's chair and stared at the desk.

"Drawers first," she told Henry. Then she opened his empty diaper bag on the floor and began dropping everything with Sara's handwriting into the bag. She took memory sticks from the middle desk drawer and the appointment book from the desktop. Anything remotely personal could be a clue, and maybe she'd see something in Sara's notes that the police hadn't. Then she might be able to give them a lead, in addition to the notebook, that would help identify Sara's abductor. Emma shuddered at the memory of the man's awful growling voice. *Who did you tell?* Her gaze jumped to Mr. Harrison's closed office door. Could he know who took her sister?

She blinked through another threat of tears.

A framed photo of Sara, Emma and their parents sat on the corner of her sister's desk. Their mom had been gone just over five years. Their dad had been gone much longer, but the holes their parents had left behind were permanent. Emma tucked the frame into her purse, unwilling to stow her parents' image with the hodgepodge of who-knew-what from Sara's desk.

Across the room Kate started back in her direction.

Emma kicked the bottom drawers shut on either side of her, then heaved the bulging diaper bag back onto her shoulder. She gave the middle drawer a shove with her free hand.

"Did you find your key?" Kate asked, coming to a stop at the cubicle's opening.

"No." Emma tipped her head and stroked Henry's fuzzy brown hair. "I guess it's lost."

"Have you checked her car?" Kate offered. "If she's anything like me, it's probably in a cup holder. I find everything from hair ties to business cards in there."

"Good idea." Emma pushed Sara's chair in when she rose, then made a show of fussing over Henry on her way out, hoping to keep Kate's eyes on her adorable baby boy instead of her suddenly crammed diaper bag.

She hurried back onto the sidewalk with a feeling of victory and rush of relief. The local marching band played their high school fight song a few blocks away, adding an excellent backdrop to her enthusiasm. They were probably entertaining at the farmer's market to raise money again, but it certainly felt personal. Emma smiled a little wider.

She arranged the too-heavy diaper bag in the crook of her arm, having nearly dislocated her shoulder with the number of note pads and notebooks she'd confiscated. "I'm going to call this a success," she told Henry, dropping a kiss onto his tiny forehead.

Heavy fingers clamped hard around her elbow. "Don't say a word, or your baby's going to take a mighty fall." A man's low voice growled in her ear. He moved into her periphery, pulling her against his side and keeping pace there.

Ice slid through Emma's veins. It was *the* voice. *Who did you tell?*

She scanned the street for Sawyer, but the man's head turned at the eruption of a bass drumline. His thick arms crossed over his chest as the marching band carried their tune to a crescendo.

A moment later, the man tugged her around the building's edge and into a small alley.

"Don't hurt him," she pleaded.

"Give the bag to me." The man moved into her view; his face was covered in a black scarf from his chin to his nose. The dark hood of his jacket hung low over his forehead.

"No." Emma needed the things in that bag. The fact he wanted the bag was a sure sign that she finally had what she needed to find Sara. "Where's my sister?"

His hand moved from her elbow to the back of her neck, compressing and squeezing until shooting pain raced up the back of her head and she cried out for him to stop. "I wasn't making a request."

He released her with a shove. "Hand over the bag, or I squeeze your baby's head next."

Emma stumbled forward, twisting at the waist to put more distance between the lunatic and her son.

Henry screamed.

The man curled meaty fingers around the straps of Henry's diaper bag and jerked hard enough to leave material burns along her forearm as it slid. Before he separated it from her completely, Emma clenched a fist around one strap. "No!" she screamed.

"Stop!" Sawyer's voice blasted through the white noise of the street beyond the alley. A heartbeat later his livid face came into view across the crowded road.

"Stop!" His eyes were fierce, and his voice boomed with authority. "Help her!" he yelled, motioning to Emma in the alley.

A few confused faces turned in her direction, gawking from the safety of the sidewalk just a few yards away.

Emma tried to hold on, tried to stall her attacker ten more seconds, just long enough for Sawyer to reach her, but the man's expression turned lethal. He reached a giant hand forward for her baby, eyes narrowed and darkening.

"No!" Emma screamed. She jerked left, spinning Henry farther away as a massive fist crashed into her cheekbone with a deafening thud. Her head snapped back and her vision blurred. Emma's knees buckled, and her back hit the brick wall of the credit union behind her. Air expelled from her lungs as she slid onto the filthy broken asphalt, Henry screaming in her arms.

The bag flew from her useless, flaccid fingers, and the man was in motion, beating a path down the alley, away from the crowd, away from Sawyer and away from Emma.

Henry wailed into her ear, arching his back in distress as Sawyer skidded to a stop at her side.

"Emma!"

She felt her strength giving way. Her arms knew to hold on, but her thoughts slipped into nothing. "Sawyer," she started, but the darkness rushed in to take her.

Chapter Four

Sawyer watched in horror as the man in black pulled back his fist and shot it forward at Emma and her baby. At *Sawyer's* baby. Fury burned in his veins, propelling him faster, erasing the final distance between them as Emma's body began to wobble and fall. She uttered Sawyer's name as his feet reached the curb only a yard from her side. The desperate, heartbreaking sound was nearly enough to land him on his knees.

Time seemed to stand still as her eyelids drooped shut, extinguishing the final glimmer of her awareness. Sawyer dove for them, catching Emma's body in a hug as it went limp and pressing both her and Henry to his chest. "Call 911!" he demanded, turning to fix a pointed look on the gathered bystanders.

Sawyer gritted his teeth as the assailant pushed through a throng of pedestrians at the alley's opposite end and escaped his wrath, for now, with Emma's bag.

The soft whir of emergency sirens spun to life in the distance, barely audible over Henry's cries.

Sawyer focused on the lives he held in his arms.

He repositioned them, allowing Emma's arms to fall to her sides, and getting a more comforting hold on Henry. "Shh," he whispered to his son. The seething anger he felt for Emma's attacker would have to wait. "I've got you, and you're going to be okay," he vowed, kissing the child's head on instinct, cuddling him tighter. And he would return the man's assaulting punch at the first opportunity.

Emma's lids fluttered open. "Henry."

"I've got him, and help is on the way for you." Sawyer took a moment to evaluate the rising bruise on her cheekbone. Her assailant's fist had been large enough to mark her from jaw to temple, and Sawyer felt his fingers curl once more with the need to return the hit. "The police and ambulance are almost here," he assured her.

The sirens were loud now. Emergency vehicles would arrive at any moment.

Then Sawyer could plot his revenge on the man who'd done this to his family.

A SLOW AND GENTLE jostling roused Emma once more. The low murmur of a crowd and distant sounds of traffic pricked her ears. A cool and hearty breeze roused her with a snap. Suddenly, Emma's muddled thoughts pulled together in a sharp and deeply horrific memory. A man had attacked her and Henry outside the credit union. He'd taken all of Sara's things. Stolen the diaper bag from her hands. *And hit her.* "Henry!" Her eyes jerked wide.

"He's here," Sawyer answered. He appeared at her side, baby tucked safely in the crook of his arm. "He's okay."

Henry worked the small blue pacifier in his mouth. A broad grin stretched beneath the little soother when he caught her in his sight.

Emma sighed in relief. "Thank you," she whispered, fighting tears and taking inventory of the changes in her situation. The assailant was gone. Sawyer was here, and she was strapped to a gurney. An EMT pressed cool, probing fingers to her wrist. "Did he get away?" she asked Sawyer, craning her neck for signs of a policeman with the lunatic in handcuffs.

"Yeah," Sawyer answered. "I'm sorry."

She shook her head. "You saved Henry."

The muscle pulsed in Sawyer's jaw. His eyes were hard and cold. "The man who hurt you got away."

Sawyer's voice raised goose bumps over her skin. His calculating expression didn't help.

"Your cheek will be tender for a while," the EMT said. He explored the red-hot ache with a gentle touch. "Skin didn't break," he said. "There's no need for a bandage or stitches, but I recommend ice for swelling and aspirin as needed for pain." He flashed a blinding light into her eyes, and she winced. "Blurry vision?" he asked.

"No."

"Memory loss?"

"No." She frowned. That wasn't completely true. "I don't remember you arriving," she said, "but I remember being cornered, robbed and assaulted by a man in head-to-toe black. He wore a scarf across the bottom half of his face."

The EMT nodded, a small frown on his lips. "I'm sorry that happened to you and your baby." He pocketed the light. "If you develop any nausea or unusual neck pain, go to the ER. Tell them about this."

"Okay," she agreed, eager to get off the gurney and avoid an ambulance ride she absolutely couldn't afford. "I can go?"

He raised his attention to Sawyer, already moving into position so he could help her down. "You'll drive her?" he asked.

Sawyer reached for Emma's hand. "Yes."

"Not so fast," a vaguely familiar voice interrupted. The detective who'd come to her home to take the report of Sara's abduction moved into view, pen and paper in hand. "I have a few questions, if you don't mind. I've spoken to several witnesses, and I'd like to get your statement as well before the details become murky from time."

Sawyer stepped between the detective and the gurney. His pale blue eyes locked onto hers. "You don't have to do this now if you don't want to. He can come by later, or I can take you to the station when you're feeling better."

Emma took a deep, settling breath and lifted her chin. "I can do it now," she said, and then she slowly relived the second-worst experience of her life in vivid detail.

When it was over, she told Detective Rosen about Sara's hidden notebook, and he promised to pick it up personally, after he'd finished with the current crime scene.

At home, she showered until her skin pruned up, attempting and failing to wash the feel of the man's hands off her. Then, with Henry dozing in his crib, she cried herself to sleep in the middle of the afternoon.

She woke to an empty crib at her bedside and the tangy scent of barbecue in the air.

She was on her feet instantly in search of her son. The scents of her grill suggested all was well, that Sawyer was grilling, but she wasn't sure she liked him nabbing Henry without letting her know. She crept down the hallway toward the kitchen warring with herself. Henry was his son, but surely common courtesy dictated that he at least let her know before taking him like that. No one else in her world would have dared. Maybe Sara. The thought clogged her throat.

Emma found Sawyer on the back porch, manning the grill as suspected.

He turned before she spoke, as if he'd somehow sensed her arrival. "Hey," he said, his gaze lingering on her cheek. "Did we wake you?"

"No," Emma said flatly, "but I wish you would have. Instead, I woke to find an empty crib. I didn't like it." Across from the grill, aligned with the porch swing she loved, Henry swung cheerfully from a red-and-yellow baby swing fastened to the rafters of the porch roof. "You put up the swing," she said, unsure if she was doubly frustrated that Sawyer had helped himself to that too, or warmed by the gesture.

Sawyer opened the lid to her steaming grill and flipped a line of burgers with practiced skill. "I found it in the garage while I was double-checking the perimeter. I think I woke the little guy with your power drill, but he let me off the hook when I suggested he give the swing a try." Pride tugged Sawyer's lips, and Emma wondered if it was his handiwork or Henry that caused it. "If you don't want the swing there, I can move it," he said, brows dipping into a V. "Whatever you want."

"It's fine," Emma said, drifting toward her son. "He clearly loves it." She stroked Henry's soft brown hair and kissed his head, inhaling the soft scents of sunshine and baby shampoo. She'd come so close to seeing him hurt today. Her fingers found the aching skin of her cheek on instinct, recalling the moment of impact with perfect, bone-rattling clarity. Then she'd been rescued by the man of her dreams. A man she'd long ago assumed had walked out of her life permanently, only to turn up and move in with her on the night of their strange reunion.

Last night.

Her stomach churned with the weight of all that had happened these last twenty-four hours. Nearly forty-eight, if she started counting from the moment her sister had been torn from their home. Her heart raced, and her mouth dried. It was just too much.

Sawyer closed the grill lid and watched her for a long beat before speaking. "Do you want to sit down?" He poured her a glass of ice water from the pitcher sitting on the little table she normally shared with Sara. "I planned to check in on you when the burgers were done. It's been a long day. I thought you might want to eat."

Emma curled one arm around her middle, attempting feebly to hold herself together. "You didn't have to do this," she said.

Sawyer gave his spatula a little spin. "It's just burgers," he said smoothly, as if that was true.

But it wasn't *just burgers*. It was the attentiveness and compassion. The protection and security. It was all the things she'd missed so deeply when Sawyer had left, and it was like peeling the scab off a wound she'd worked very hard to heal.

Emma straightened her spine. "I meant you don't have to watch Henry so I can sleep or hang swings or cook for me." The gestures were clearly meant to be helpful and not intrusive, she decided, and she couldn't be mad that he'd taken Henry from the crib when he woke. It was a fatherly thing to do. The swing. The burgers. All acts of kindness. But Emma's gut still churned with anger. She didn't need Sawyer's help with those things. She'd been fine on her own all these months. Why should he get to walk back in and pretend he'd been here all along?

Sawyer narrowed his eyes. "It's the least I can do, don't you think?"

"No," she said honestly. "I called Fortress Security because I needed help keeping Henry safe and finding Sara. You saved us from that lunatic today. That's what I need from you. That and help finding my sister."

Sawyer's eyes went cold at the mention of the man in the alley. It was a new look on him. One she wasn't sure she'd ever get used to. "How are you feeling?" he asked.

"My face hurts," she said. "I'm mad in general. I'm also thankful Henry wasn't hurt."

Sawyer took a step in her direction, hand raised as if he might touch her swollen cheek. He stopped short, clearly thinking better of it, and lowered his arm. He raised his attention from the bruise to her eyes. "I'm going to find the man who did this."

"Good, because I think he was the same man who took Sara," she said through a tightening throat, "and that man is a monster."

"What?" Sawyer's already aggravated expression darkened. "Are you sure?"

She nodded. "I recognized his voice. So, I can tell you from experience that Henry and I were lucky. I stood by and listened as he strangled Sara with his bare hands, held her down, made her bleed, then dragged her away." The memory of mopping her sister's blood off the living room floor rushed back to mind, and she stood, ready to run. She didn't want to have an emotional breakdown in front of Henry. Or Sawyer. The day had been too difficult already. "Excuse me."

Sawyer was on his feet instantly. "Hey." He caught her in his arms and pulled her against his chest. The strong, familiar embrace felt so much like home, so much like everything she'd been missing for far too long. "I know I wasn't here for you before," he said, "but I'm here now, and I'm not going anywhere. You're not alone, Emma." He stroked her hair, and her heart gave a heavy thump.

She tried not to read into his promise. He wasn't going anywhere *for now*, but he'd be gone again when Sara came home. He would stay in Henry's life after that, but not in hers. Not really. Not the way her twisting heart wanted. Tears pricked her eyes, and her chest grew heavy with the need to cry.

"Excuse me," she blurted, bobbing free of him and running back inside.

Tears streamed over her cheeks with every footstep down the long hall to her room.

SAWYER KNOCKED ON Emma's door a few minutes later, then swung it open. The en suite bathroom door was ajar. "Emma?" he called. "Everything okay?"

She stepped out of the bathroom with red-rimmed eyes and blotchy skin. "Sorry. I needed a minute."

Sawyer set Henry in the crib beside her bed, a fresh cocktail of anger and regret mixing in his gut. "Feeling better?"

"No." She blew out a shaky breath, checking the corners of her mouth with her fingertips. "Not much. How's Henry?"

Sawyer gave his son a quick look. "He conked out in the swing. I wasn't sure it was good for him to sleep with his head tipped the way it was."

"Thanks." She moved toward the crib, toward Henry, and the urge to pull her against him was nearly too much.

He shoved his hands into his pockets. "You know that what happened to Sara isn't your fault," he said. "You couldn't have fought that guy and protected Henry at the same time. You did the only thing you could do. You were smart, quick thinking and brave."

"I don't feel like any of those things," she said, dragging her gaze from Henry to Sawyer.

He understood. Better than she could know. "Well, do you feel like a burger?"

Emma nodded, and Sawyer led her to the kitchen, where he'd set the table in her absence. She took a seat and downed the glass of ice water he'd poured for her. "How'd everything look when you checked the property?"

"Could be better," he said, hoping to sound less frustrated than he had been at the sight of the inadequate security measures protecting two single women and a baby. "Your locks are old. The windows are old. There are no security cameras. No alarm." He ran a heavy hand over his head and gripped the back of his neck. "I'll replace the locks and see what I can do to better secure the windows."

Emma set her empty glass aside and frowned. "I'd hoped to raise Henry on a farm, not inside a fortress."

"We all hope for a lot of things," Sawyer said stiffly. "But we have to adapt to the situations at hand, and right now, you need a fortress."

Emma placed a burger on her plate and covered it in mushrooms and onions, going through the motions, he assumed, but forgoing the bun.

Sawyer made his burger and bit into it, keeping one eye on her. He'd grilled burgers for her a dozen times during their monthlong whirlwind romance. In fact, some of his favorite memories with Emma had a grill in the background.

He'd been given a thirty-day leave last year after a particularly intense and dangerous mission, and he'd only expected to sleep in and veg out. Instead, he'd met Emma at a bonfire near a lake where he'd been fishing. He'd marched over to her, introduced himself. They'd hit it off, and he begged for her number when it was time for her to leave. He called her as she walked away. Invited her to fireworks in the park the next night. They'd spent nearly every day together from there. Until he had to go back.

Emma pushed the veggies around with her fork. "What if we don't find her?" she asked, pulling his thoughts back to the present.

Sawyer paused, the burger partway to his lips. "We'll find her."

"How do you know?"

"Because it's what I do. I search and rescue. I find people who don't want to be found, and I bring folks who are desperate to be found home." Images of his last mission flashed into mind. He'd taken his men on a rescue mission with bad intel. He'd assessed the risk, and he'd been dead wrong. He walked them into a trap, and that had cost five good men their lives. It darn near cost Sawyer his sanity.

"What if we find her and it's too late when we do?" The quaver in Emma's voice opened Sawyer's eyes. He hadn't realized he'd shut them.

Sawyer put the burger down. "We're going to find Sara, and she's going to be okay when we do," he promised. "Meanwhile, I'll be here to make sure no one gets near you or Henry again while we figure out what was going on. Okay?"

Emma shook her head, looking half-ill and pursing her lips.

"What?" he asked. They'd just covered her safety, Henry's safety and Sara's safe return. What else could make her look that way?

"I let go of the bag," she said. "I had everything from Sara's desk in that bag, and I let him have it."

"You didn't let him have anything," Sawyer argued. "I watched you fight him for it while holding a baby."

Emma shook her head. "Now he has what he wanted, and he doesn't have a reason to keep her alive anymore. Letting go of that bag might've killed my sister."

"Whoa." Sawyer raised his hands into a T for a time-out. "Look. You don't know any of that. Not his motivation. Not his endgame. You don't even know if what he wanted was in that bag. If he wanted the notebook with the numbers, the joke is on him because we had that and Detective Rosen picked it up an hour ago as promised."

Emma lifted hopeful eyes to his. "Yeah."

"Yeah," he said.

She nodded, steadying herself. "You're right." She forked a stack of mushrooms, studying them, her thoughts clearly somewhere else.

"Spill it," Sawyer said, wiping his mouth and then pressing the napkin to the table. "I've been gone awhile, but I know that face. You've got something to say. So, say it. It's better to clear the air than try to work through the smoke. Heaven knows we've got little fires burning everywhere."

She leaned forward, elbows on the table. "How did you get through the things you went through overseas? I know you're trained. You're smart. You're tough. That's not what I mean."

Sawyer bit into his burger, locked in her gaze and wishing she knew it was memories of her that had gotten him through the worst things imaginable. "Hope."

Emma pushed a forkful of mushrooms into her mouth and watched him curiously. She nodded. "I can do that." She chewed, swallowed, had some water, still scrutinizing Sawyer until he itched to get up and move. Her gaze shifted quickly away before returning to meet his. "I spent a lot of time over the past year wondering if you ever thought of me," she said, cheeks reddening.

He could see the honesty cost her. So, he would be honest right back. "I did. Often. I used to think of the things we'd done together. Now I'm just thinking about all the things I've missed." He clamped his mouth shut and did his best to look less vulnerable than he suddenly felt. Things were complicated enough between him and Emma without him getting emotional. This wasn't the time for heart-to-hearts and personal confessions.

The mission was to find Sara and protect Emma and Henry at all costs. He took another angrier bite of burger.

Emma stood and left.

Sawyer groaned. He used to be a people person. He made people comfortable, at ease, even happy. Lately, he could clear a room with a look and a greeting. He hadn't particularly minded the change until now.

Emma returned several minutes later with a scrapbook. She set it on the table beside his plate. "Sara made this for me."

She returned to her seat and lifted her fork to finish dinner.

Sawyer examined the big blue book. Henry's

name and newborn photo were glued to the cover
and framed with red ribbon. A photo of Emma in a
ponytail and "baby on board" T-shirt was positioned
just below the first. Her beautifully round belly was
tough to look away from, and it hit him again. She'd
been pregnant. Delivered their child. Brought him
home. Got to know him. Learned to care for him,
and Sawyer had missed it all.

He opened the book and turned the pages with
reverence, poring over every detail. Every photo.
Every inscription. He admired the proud smile on
Emma's face in each photo.

"What's wrong?" Emma asked, resting back in
her chair. "You look furious."

"No." He closed the book. A swell of pride and
gratitude expanded his chest. "Thank you," he said
softly.

She quirked a brow. "You can't keep that. Sara
made it for me."

"No." He laughed. "Not for the book. For Henry."

Emma's cheeks reddened again. "It's not like I
made him on my own."

"No, but you did everything else on your own,"
he said. "I can't imagine how frightening it was to
learn you were going to have a baby. Especially one
whose father was literally MIA." He thought again of
the monsters who'd taken those months and his men
from him, but forced the images aside. He curled his
fingers around the book's edge, grounding himself
to the present. "You could've chosen so many other

ways to deal with your pregnancy, and I swear I never would've judged you, whatever you'd decided, but—" he cleared his thickening throat "—but because you made these choices—" he lifted the scrapbook in a white-knuckle grip "—I'm a father, and whatever you think of me now, I am irrevocably indebted to you for this."

Emma's mouth fell open, then was slowly pulled shut. "You're welcome."

Sawyer's aching heart warmed at her acceptance of his apology. It was a step in the right direction. "What was it like?" he asked.

"Scary at first, then pretty amazing," she said, forking a bite of bunless burger into her mouth. "I got really fat."

Sawyer let his gaze trail over her, indulging himself in the admiration of her new curves. "Agree to disagree."

"I'm working on getting back in shape now," she assured him. "It feels good but getting chubby with a purpose was fun too." Her lips twitched, nearly accomplishing a smile.

By the time dinner was done, and Sawyer had cleared the table, some of the smoky air between them had cleared, as well. Emma joined him at the sink in companionable silence as they washed and dried dishes by hand before putting them away. It was dangerously easy to be with Emma when she wasn't looking at him as if *he* might be the one in need of protection *from her*. Easy to let himself think there could a future for them, that he could somehow make up for his absence when it had counted most.

But Sawyer couldn't afford to think that way. Couldn't afford to get distracted until he brought Sara home safely as promised. Only after he'd proved himself worthy of Emma's trust would he allow himself to dream of more. Until then, he had work to do.

Chapter Five

Sawyer's eyes snapped open, his senses on alert. According to the clock on Emma's living room wall, it was approaching 3:00 a.m., meaning he'd slept for four straight hours. It was the longest stretch he'd managed since returning stateside, and he felt unnervingly vulnerable for it.

Normally he woke to the screams of his fallen teammates or the pain of his own torture, but not this time. So, what had woken him?

He tuned in to the quiet home, suddenly acutely aware that it was his gut that had jerked him into the moment. *Instinct.* His pulse quickened as he listened. For what? He wasn't sure. Sawyer straightened, planted his feet silently on the floor.

The baby monitor on the coffee table caught his eye. He waited for an indication that Henry had stirred and woken Sawyer, but there was only the slow and steady breaths of a sleeping child.

"Sawyer?" Emma whispered, struggling upright on the couch, where she'd fallen asleep midsentence during the retelling of a pregnancy story. He'd been wholly engrossed in the details, but her words had turned to soft snores before she'd finished, and he hadn't had the heart to wake her or the guts to try to move her. He certainly had no right to touch her.

She frowned in the dark. "What's wrong?"

He considered telling her everything was fine, but he hadn't had time to confirm that yet, and the distinct creak of floorboards removed the possibility it was true.

Her eyes stretched wide. "Someone's in the house?" She flicked her gaze to the baby monitor, and panic drained the blood from her face.

Sawyer lifted a finger to his lips, then reached for his sidearm, tucked carefully between the cushion and overstuffed arm of Emma's chair where he'd rested. Then he reached for her. Much as he didn't want to bring her into harm's way, he couldn't afford to leave her alone either.

Emma followed closely on his heels, her small hands at his waist as they crept down the hall toward the sound.

Each bedroom door was open as they passed. Each light off. The laundry room. The guest bedroom, where Sawyer's things were stashed. Emma's room, where Henry slept soundly, unaware of the intruder or his parents' fears.

At her bedroom door, Emma released Sawyer and stepped over the threshold. She shot a pleading gaze at him, and he nodded before pulling the door shut with her inside.

He waited for the soft snick of the lock before moving on.

The bathroom door was open also. A night-light illuminated the narrow space, projecting the silhouette of a duck onto one wall.

When Sawyer reached Sara's room, the door was closed.

A beam of light flashed along the floor inside, leaking into the hallway at his feet. A sly grin slid over Sawyer's mouth. He hadn't imagined an opportunity to return the man's punch so soon, but he was glad for it, and unlike Emma, this guy wouldn't be waking up so soon after the hit.

Sawyer cast a look over his shoulder, confirming he was still alone, and he hoped Emma had taken Henry to hide wherever they'd gone the night Sara was taken. Someplace she could call the police and wait safely until help arrived.

He struck a defensive position behind the closed door and turned the doorknob carefully. The soldier in him rose instinctively and unbidden. His mind and muscles falling instantly on their training.

The door swung on noisy hinges, and the creaking of floorboards turned quickly into the loud groan and rattle of an aged wooden window frame forced upward faster than it was prepared to go.

"Not on my watch," Sawyer said, flipping the

light on and aiming his gun toward the window. "Stop right there."

A man in all black looked at him from the bedroom window, one half of his body still inside the room as he straddled the casing, a black duffel bag over his shoulder.

"Release the bag and climb back inside slowly," Sawyer demanded, hyperaware that only one of the intruder's hands was visible from this angle.

The man shifted the duffel from his shoulder to his palm and stretched it into the room toward Sawyer.

"Drop it," Sawyer barked. "Now, show me your other hand."

The man dipped his chin slowly. His opposite hand came into view with a gun poised to shoot.

"Put your weapon down." Sawyer's voice slid into the deep authoritative timbre that forced most folks to obey his commands. This man didn't budge.

"I *will* shoot you," Sawyer warned. "I'm willing to bet my aim is better than yours." He let his mouth curve into a sinister smile, enjoying the weight and feel of his SIG Sauer against his palm and the flash of indecision on the man's face.

Henry's scream broke the silent standoff and Sawyer's concentration. A million terrifying scenarios thundered through his brain like a punch to his gut. Was there a second intruder? Had Sawyer overlooked him? Was Henry hurt? Was Emma?

The intruder's gun went off with a deafening bang!

Sawyer jumped back into the hall, pressing himself to the wall and cursing inwardly at the moment of distraction. "Emma!" he called.

Henry cried again, but Emma didn't answer.

Sawyer swore. He spun silently back into Sara's bedroom, already aiming for the window. He pulled his trigger as the muffled thud of the duffel bag hit the ground outside. The man took a second wild shot at Sawyer, then toppled out the open window, smearing blood over the frame and Sara's wall beneath.

Sawyer's attention stuck to the hole in the drywall a few feet away from his head. The intruder's final shot had missed him by several feet, but the hole had punched through a wall shared with Sara's room. A wall shared by Henry and his crib.

EMMA'S PULSE BEAT in her ears as she burrowed deeper into the walk-in closet that had been her refuge just two nights before. She could only pray it would be enough to protect her again. She shushed her fussing baby and tried desperately not to imagine Sawyer being injured while she hid. She couldn't live knowing another loved one had been taken from her while she sat idly by, but what could she do? She couldn't leave Henry, and she wouldn't risk making him an orphan, so she was stuck. Hiding and waiting. And praying. Again.

The dispatch officer insisted on staying on the line with her until the police arrived. "Can you see anything from your location?" she asked.

"No," Emma whispered. "Please hurry."

"What can you hear?" the dispatcher asked. "Can you tell me the number of intruders based on voices?"

Emma shook her head, unsure she could make another sound even if she wanted. Even if she wasn't terrified her voice would give away her hiding spot and put her baby in danger.

"Ma'am," the dispatcher began again, but a sudden gunshot reverberated through the silent home, stopping her midinterrogation.

Emma's heart seized and her chest constricted.

"Was that gunfire?" the dispatch officer asked abruptly, concern in her voice.

"I—" Emma nodded. "Yes." She stroked Henry's hair as he began to scream once more. "Help us," she breathed. "Please."

The blast that erupted next poured tears onto her cheeks.

Henry's eyes were wide in the glow from her phone. His lips pulled low into a full pout, startled to silence by the sound but ready to wail at any moment.

"Was anyone hurt? Do you need an ambulance?" the dispatcher demanded.

"I don't know." She covered her mouth with one palm to stifle a building sob.

The door to her room banged open, and she screamed. The door ricocheted against the wall, rattling the closet where she hid. "Henry!" Sawyer yelled. "Emma!"

A wave of relief pressed the air from her lungs.

"Here," she croaked. "We're here." She inched forward as the closet door opened, balancing a crying Henry in her arms and the phone against her shoulder.

Sawyer dropped to his knees and pulled them into his arms. "Thank goodness." He took Henry from her, then offered a hand to pull her to her feet. "Call 911," he instructed. "I shot the intruder, but he got away with a duffel bag. I don't know what was in it."

Emma lifted the phone from her shoulder. "They're on the way."

He closed his eyes for a long beat, then reopened them to kiss Henry's hair and round cheeks a dozen times before kissing Emma's forehead and pulling her close. "May I?" he asked, sliding a hand up to take the phone. He spoke heatedly with Dispatch for several moments while Emma stepped away.

Her insides fluttered and her limbs quaked with excess adrenaline as she tried to follow Sawyer's explanation of what had happened inside Sara's room.

"I definitely hit him. There's blood. He'll need a hospital," Sawyer said.

A dark spot on the wall caught Emma's attention, and she moved across her room to inspect it through the bars of Henry's crib. A hole in the drywall. Inches from the place where Henry laid his head at night. She touched the hole with shaking fingers, and nausea rolled in her stomach. "He could be dead," she whispered.

Sawyer opened a pocketknife and dug the casing from the wall with his handkerchief. "I've got the brass," he said. "This might be all we need to track him. We can match the gun if it's registered. Match the print if he's in the system."

Flashers lit the world outside her bedroom window.

"Cavalry's here," he told Dispatch, pulling the curtain back for a look into the driveway.

Sawyer returned the phone to Emma, then headed for the front door with Henry to greet the emergency responders.

Emma tried not to look too long or hard at the crib or the bullet hole in the wall at its side. She doubted she'd ever be able to lay Henry there again, and she was sure she wouldn't sleep if she did.

She followed them to the living room, Henry lodged tightly against Sawyer's chest, silent and calm. Shocking because Henry wasn't good with strangers. Though Sawyer wasn't really a stranger, she thought. Sawyer was his father.

She took Henry from him as he greeted the line of police officers, crime scene officials and the detective she'd spoken to earlier that day. She didn't have it in her to speak without crying, and tears would help nothing. Coffee, on the other hand, cured a multitude of things, and she could make a pot to be useful.

She moved to the kitchen as men and women in uniforms canvassed her home. There wouldn't be any more sleeping for her tonight, but honestly, she wasn't sure how she'd ever sleep again.

Sawyer paused outside the kitchen as a pair of

uniforms passed by. "You okay?" he asked, concern and compassion plain in the words and his expression.

"Mmm-hmm." She nodded, pushing her attention back to the chore at hand.

Tonight's gunshots had punctured more than the drywall. The possibility she'd lost Sawyer again had wrenched her heart in agony and eradicated her carefully constructed walls of emotional protection. The realization that he was safe but would leave once Sara was home, made her chest pinch and ache in the extreme. She wasn't sure what that meant, but she was nearly positive it wouldn't end well for her raw and aching heart.

Chapter Six

Emma set Henry in his high chair once he'd calmed from the scare and offered him his favorite teether. At just over four months, his coordination wasn't great, but once he got the rubber cactus to his mouth, he normally chewed happily. Tonight was no different, and Emma marveled at the resilience of her son. If only she could suck it up so easily and move on to the moment at hand.

She turned to the counter and rubbed trembling palms down the legs of her jeans. Brewing the coffee and setting out the cups, cream and sugar would give her an outlet for the energy surplus buzzing around inside her.

Sawyer appeared a moment later, leaning against the jamb. "How are you holding up?"

"Not as well as Henry," she said, "but I suppose I should expect as much from your son." She poured a mug of coffee and extended it in Sawyer's direction. "Coffee?"

Sawyer accepted the mug. He took a long pull

on the steaming drink, eyes focused on her. "You did great tonight," he said. "With everything going on, I forgot to say that sooner, but it's true. Henry's a lucky kid."

Emma nodded woodenly. What had she done besides hide? *Again.* She was sick of being caught off guard and forced to react to all the villainous encounters. She wanted to *do* something that would stop them. Not hide until the situations passed. "We need to find out what he was looking for," she said. "It was a good sign. If whatever he wanted wasn't in the bag of things I took from her office, then Sara might still be alive."

Sawyer gave one stiff dip of his chin.

"If he found whatever he'd been after in her room tonight, then we don't have much time," she said. "We have to do something."

Detective Rosen arrived in the kitchen behind Sawyer. "Do I smell coffee?"

Sawyer nodded. "Help yourself."

The detective poured a cup, then offered Emma his hand. "I'm sorry to be back so soon, Miss Hart. I understand you were able to contact Dispatch while staying out of danger's path and protecting your son to boot. Nice work."

"Any word on Sara's whereabouts?" Emma asked, ignoring the comment about her spectacular abilities to hide and use a telephone.

"I'm sorry," Rosen said. "Not yet. We're running

down every lead, but we don't have anything to share at the moment."

"Well, which is it?" she asked, working to control her tone and not upset Henry again. "Is there nothing to share or just nothing you're willing to share?"

The detective looked at Sawyer, who returned his level gaze. "Nothing worth sharing," he said.

"Try me," Emma dared. "You'd be surprised how little it would take to reassure me right now."

Detective Rosen rocked back on his heels and cleared his throat. "Well, we're working on the theory that this had something to do with her position at the credit union," he began. "We're unclear how her job and the abduction are related, but we believe they are."

Emma's hopes sank. She'd hoped the leads he'd mentioned were significant. Maybe even inside tips of some sort. Instead, it sounded like the police didn't have anything more than she'd come up with on her own.

Sawyer moved to her side, silently sharing his strength with her. "Any luck on deciphering the notebook's contents?"

"Not yet." Detective Rosen set his empty mug aside and fixed Emma with a patient look. "Mr. Lance said the intruder took a duffel bag with him. Do you think you might be able to walk through the room and tell me what's missing?"

Emma stepped away from Sawyer and pulled Henry from his high chair with a kiss. "I didn't spend much time in Sara's room," she said, moving into the hall behind the detective. "I'm not sure I'd notice if anything was missing besides the furniture, but I'll try."

A handful of men in various uniforms filled the space inside her sister's room, dusting the window frame for prints, taking photos and collecting blood from the floor.

Emma inched inside. Her pulse quickened and her breaths grew shallow. Seeing the policemen and crime scene people picking through Sara's things was like losing her all over again. The blood on the wall and windowsill reminded her of the broad smear she'd cleaned off the living room floor.

"Hey." Sawyer moved in front of her, the toes of his shoes bumping hers. "Take your time."

She snuggled Henry tighter and forced her gaze around the room. The items on Sara's vanity, bookcase and nightstand were scattered. The floor was covered with the contents of her closet. Her mattress was askew from the box spring. "Maybe if I clean up," she said. "It's too messy right now. I don't know where to look."

"All right," the detective said. "We're almost done. You can let us know once you've had time to reorganize." He handed Sawyer a business card, then drifted back down the hallway.

More than an hour later, the house was finally, eerily still.

Sawyer double-checked the door lock, then turned to face her. "What do you want to do?" he asked.

She shook her head, heartbroken and mystified. "I have no idea."

He pulled a set of keys from his pocket and raised them beside his handsome face. "Why don't we get out of here?"

HE DIDN'T HAVE to ask Emma twice. When he'd offered to take her and Henry to his place for a while, she'd packed two bags without hesitation. Inside the cab of his truck, Emma watched her family ranch until it was swallowed by distance and darkness.

"What are you thinking?" he asked when the curiosity became too much.

"I don't know where you live," she said with a small laugh. "I was thinking that two days ago I would never have agreed to go home with someone without asking where they lived."

Sawyer locked his jaw against the complaint that he wasn't just someone. He was Henry's father, a man she'd called in to protect her and someone she'd once claimed to have loved.

She fiddled with the hem of her shirt. "I suppose you don't still live on base with four other rangers."

"No," he said. "They tend to cut off our housing once we're discharged." He glanced her way across the dimly lit cab. "I bought a place in the next county. We won't be more than an hour away if the police call with new information and you want to get back."

Emma turned curious eyes on him. "Where in the next county?"

"Lake Anna," he said, nearly crushed by a wave of nostalgia.

She swiveled in her seat, eyes wide with interest. They'd met at Lake Anna, and Emma had loved visiting the lake when they'd dated. She told him once that she wanted to live there someday, and he'd promised to buy her a home with a dock and lots of privacy so they could make love under the stars anytime they wanted. Sawyer assumed the rising color in her cheeks meant that she hadn't forgotten that conversation either.

He checked the rearview mirror as they moved along the desolate highway, one of only a few dozen cars traveling just before dawn. He passed his exit and got off on an unlit, extremely rural ramp instead, checking again for signs they'd been followed. By the time he backtracked several miles and made a few unnecessary turns to confirm they were still alone, the sun was rising.

Emma straightened and rubbed her eyes as they bounced down the pitted gravel lane to his simple A-frame cottage. The motion light snapped on as he settled the vehicle outside, welcoming him home. The lawn was still dark, shaded by the surrounding forest, but the lake before them was the color of fire, reflecting the sunrise over its glassy surface.

Sawyer bypassed the wide parking area near his back porch in favor of a smaller, narrower patch of gravel near the home's side entrance. He used this door as his front door, because the actual front of his home faced the lake.

Sawyer climbed out and grabbed Emma's things from the back, then met her on the passenger side. He took Henry's bulbous car seat carrier from her hands. "You'll be safe here," he promised, stepping onto the wide wraparound porch. "We weren't followed, and I've barely moved in, so even if the man I shot managed to get my name somehow, the only people who know where I live are my teammates in Lexington. The home is technically owned by the company, for privacy reasons, so it will take some time and know-how to track us here."

He unlocked the door and hit the light switch inside, then motioned for Emma to pass. Sawyer keyed in the code to the silent alarm system, then caught Emma's eye as she took the place in.

She folded her arms and made a circuit around the living room, stopping to look at the photos on his mantel, then out the stretch of windows facing the lake.

Sawyer set Henry's car seat near the couch and went to join her. "What do you think?"

"It's beautiful," she said.

"Thanks." He gave the space a critical exam. Packed boxes filled the corners. Stacks of paint cans and piles of new fixtures lined the walls and nearly every flat surface. He'd gotten the place at a steal, planning to use it as a safe house for Fortress until he fell in love with it. Unable to separate the cabin and its location from his memories with Emma, he'd decided to move in. That decision had led to a lot of unexpected work and added costs. Like updating *everything* and getting the place a mailbox and address. For the past fifty or so years, it had been little more than a cabin in the woods. Someplace someone had built to spend weekends, but never intended as a home. "It needs a lot of work, but they say it's all about location, right?"

"That's what they say," she said softly, still focused on the lake and rising sun. "I can't believe you've been this close and I had no idea."

Sawyer had thought the same thing the moment she'd told him he had a son. He was just one county line away, and he'd still missed the kid's entire life so far.

"How's Cade?" she asked his reflection in the glass. "I've been so wrapped up in my messes that I haven't even thought to ask you about your little brother."

Sawyer smiled at their reflections, side by side in his new home. "Cade's good. He's finishing up with the Marines soon, and he'll join Fortress when he gets out."

"Sounds like your security firm has become the family business." She nodded appreciatively, a note of pride in her voice. "You had your doubts about going big right out of the army, but I knew," she said. "I've always known you could do anything."

Sawyer stepped closer and put his hands back

into his pockets to stop them from reaching for her. "Wyatt put everything in motion." Sawyer had been scheduled for discharge with Wyatt, his closest friend and brother in arms, but his captivity had kept him from it and forced Wyatt to do everything on his own. Another case of Sawyer leaving loved ones to fend for themselves.

Wyatt, like Emma, had done a fine job without him.

Emma erased the final few inches between them, bringing her foot and leg flush with his. She linked her arm through his and tipped her head against his shoulder.

Sawyer raised the opposite arm across his chest and set his hand over hers on his arm.

Soon the sun gleamed orange and was well above the horizon, looking as if it might have risen from the fiery water's depths. Sawyer couldn't resist it any longer. He slid the patio door open and ushered Emma outside. She gave their sleeping son a glance before moving onto the deck, where Sawyer had spent every early morning since he'd moved in. If there was an upside to insomnia, it was that he never missed a sunrise.

"Where are all the other lake houses?" Emma asked, scanning the scene in both directions. "I remember there being so many."

"Those are closer to town. We're on a finger of the lake, tucked between a privately owned hundred-acre property and the national forest."

"Wow." She pushed a strand of windblown hair behind her ear and surveyed the scene again, this time with a look of remarkable appreciation. Pride swelled nonsensically in Sawyer's chest once more. Her approval of his home probably meant more to him than it should, but he didn't care, he liked it.

Emma turned to him; there seemed to be a question in her eyes, but she didn't ask it. "I should set up Henry's crib," she said. "I hate to see him sleeping in the car seat." She headed back inside and lifted the portable crib off the floor where Sawyer had left it. "Where do you want us?"

Sawyer bit his tongue against the truth, that he wanted her and Henry right there, with him permanently, but he knew that wasn't what she'd meant, and it was much too soon, not to mention unfair, to spring something like that on her. What he needed to do was find Sara. Complete the mission. Prove himself.

He showed Emma to the spare room across the hall from his, and watched as she expertly unpacked and set up the portable crib, then changed Henry and got him back to sleep with only the smallest cry of protest. She really was great at being a mother. His son was a lucky boy.

Sawyer's father had been a real son of a gun, and Sawyer had sworn long ago to never repeat any of his varied and extensive mistakes. *If* he ever had a family of his own. He'd already started off on the wrong foot by not returning Emma's calls. Even if he thought he was doing her a favor. He should've let her make that decision for herself. Now he could only hope that she'd forgive him. She might understand logically why he hadn't called, but the pain of feeling rejected and unwanted was a lot to overcome, and there was nothing logical about the process.

"Sawyer?" Emma asked, pulling him from his reverie. "Are you going to lie down awhile?"

"No." He bristled at the thought. He had far too much to protect under his roof now, and too much work to be done in the meanwhile. "I'm going to have another look at Sara's notebook."

Emma crossed her arms and frowned. "I thought you gave it to Detective Rosen."

He nodded. "I did. Right after I photographed the pages."

She smiled. "Okay. I'm not sure I'll be able to sleep, but I'm going to try. Once Henry wakes, he'll need me."

"Of course." Sawyer moved toward the door, longing to tell her she wasn't alone. She didn't have to carry the weight of single parenthood anymore. He could make bottles, change diapers, shake rattles. He was hardly a professional at those things, but he was a quick study and he wanted to learn. Instead, he settled for "I'll be here if you need me."

Emma curled her small hand over his on the doorknob. "Thank you," she said softly.

Sawyer's body stiffened at her touch, with the urge to pull her against him and kiss her the way he'd dreamed of doing for a year. "For what?"

"For coming to my rescue the other night. For protecting us now." She removed her hand from his and slid her palm up the length of his arm and over his shoulder. When her fingers reached the back of his neck, a firestorm of electricity coursed through him.

She rocked onto her toes and kissed his cheek. "Good night."

Sawyer nodded once, then pulled the bedroom door shut between them while he could still bring himself to walk away.

EMMA WOKE HOURS later to the sound of Henry's laughter.

Her bedroom door was open and his portable crib was empty, but his laugh was brightening her day even before her feet had hit the floor. According to her phone, it was nearly lunchtime. She'd had more sleep than she'd expected, given the circumstances, and she felt almost hopeful as she padded down the hall of Sawyer's lake house toward the living area.

The sliding patio doors were open, and Sawyer was on the porch swing with Henry, a near repeat of a similar situation yesterday. Funny the difference a day made. Emma couldn't find it in her to be irritated now. A cool breeze blew off the lake, tousling her hair as she emerged onto the wide wooden planks and joined them. "Sounds like you guys are having a good time."

"We are," Sawyer answered. "We've already been down to the dock to feed the ducks and fish," he said.

"Henry had a bottle and is on his third diaper. It's been a busy morning."

Emma stroked her son's cheek. "When did you learn to make bottles and change diapers?" she asked, enjoying the warm, easy smile on Sawyer's face. He looked at ease, even peaceful, holding Henry to his chest.

"YouTube," he said. "I considered asking you for instructions, but I didn't want to wake you."

"Well, that was one way to do it." Emma smiled at the sunlight winking across the water. She'd always wanted a place just like this one, and Sawyer had found one, complete with a boat dock and canoe. Now here they were, in the place they'd wanted to be, but time and circumstance had changed everything. Was there a way back for them, after all they'd been through? The electricity continually zinging in the air between them suggested there was, but was chemistry enough? She had Henry to think about now.

"I made coffee if you need a pick-me-up," Sawyer said. "Creamer's in the refrigerator if you want it."

"Thanks." She turned for the house, suddenly desperate for the caffeine.

Sawyer stood with Henry. "Why don't we make lunch and watch the twelve o'clock news? Maybe there will be coverage of Sara's disappearance. Cops can be tight-lipped, but reporters rarely are."

Emma nodded. "Good idea."

Sawyer beat her to the refrigerator and passed her the creamer. "How about BLTs?"

"Sounds good." She poured the coffee while Sawyer made the sandwiches and Henry bobbed in his portable high chair, attached to the side of Sawyer's table. She scanned the utilitarian space and smiled. Sawyer's decorating style was a clear reflection of himself. The only valuable items in sight were above the fireplace. In the event of a robbery, the television was the best a thief would do here. In case of a fire, Sawyer would go straight for the line of framed photos below the flat screen. She pulled her purse off the back of the chair and dug inside for another priceless photo and carried it to the mantel. "Do you mind?" she asked, setting the picture of her parents with her and Sara in line beside Sawyer's photos. "I took it from Sara's desk and put it in my purse for safekeeping. Luckily, that psychopath didn't get it when he took the diaper bag."

Sawyer moved into the space behind her and powered on the television. The heat from his torso warmed her chest as he reached around her. "You can put anything of yours anywhere you like around here."

She let herself lean back and rest against him a moment before returning to the kitchen. She had to stay focused. Had to remember what was at stake. Sara was missing, and that was why Sawyer was there, not to fulfill some long-suffering fantasy of Emma's. Her heart was already a mess of tattered shreds without giving in to a desire that would only leave her hollow and ruined.

Sawyer set the table, and they settled in to a quiet meal of chips and sandwiches when the local news began.

"Do you think they'll mention the break-in at my place last night?" she asked. "Or my mugging outside the credit union?" Did the whole town know what she was going through?

A woman in a gray pantsuit stood before the camera. "Here at the scene of an early-morning hit-and-run on Main Street," she began.

"A hit-and-run," Emma groaned. "What is going on in our town lately? Has everyone gone mad?"

Sawyer's eyes narrowed, but he didn't move his attention from the television. He lifted the remote and pumped the volume up to ten. "That looks like Sara's credit union in the background."

"What?" Emma set her sandwich aside and peered more closely at the flat screen over the fireplace.

"According to authorities," the reporter continued, "assistant branch manager Kate Brisbane was on her way to work this morning when a white sedan struck and threw her, leaving Kate with extensive injuries. She was taken by ambulance to Mercy General Hospital, where doctors have admitted her to the ICU for treatment and observation."

Emma covered her mouth with both hands. She'd just spoken to Kate yesterday before she was cornered outside the credit union, mugged and hit.

Kate's accident couldn't have been a coincidence. Could it? She turned her gaze to Sawyer, who was still glaring at the television.

"Kate Brisbane is the one you spoke with yesterday before you were assaulted?" he asked.

"Yes."

He pushed to his feet, plate in hand. "You want to go to the hospital?" he asked. "Pretend to be family so we can talk to Kate and see if she remembers anything more than the color of the car that hit her?"

"Absolutely."

Chapter Seven

Emma fought her surging emotions all the way to the hospital. The last few days were taking a toll on her both mentally and physically. Any one of the things she was experiencing would normally have been enough to keep her busy overthinking for weeks. Piling them up day after day without a moment to breath or process was making her half-ill, jittery and desperate for a break.

Sawyer watched his mirrors diligently, his gaze making a continual circuit from rearview, to sideview, to the road, then back again. She presumed the exercise was to be sure they weren't being followed, and for roughly the thousandth time since Sawyer's arrival, she was struck with overwhelming gratitude to have him there with her.

He followed the hospital signs to visitor parking without a word, then helped her out of the truck before reaching for Henry's car seat. "Are you ready for this?" he asked.

"Not really," she admitted. She hadn't been ready

for any of it, but here she was. She took Sawyer's arm as he beeped the doors locked on the truck and turned for the hospital entrance. She tried not to imagine they were a real family as passersby smiled at them. Though it was certainly a nice thought.

She let her mind slip past the reminder that this was only temporary as she stepped through the hospital's automatic doors, and she refocused on the reason they were there. Someone had tried to kill Kate this morning, and anything Kate could remember might be the key to finding Sara.

Sawyer hit the elevator button, and the doors parted. He scanned the partial list of floors and wards as Emma boarded ahead of him. She hit the number six when he stepped in behind her.

"How do you know which floor the ICU is on?" he asked.

"It's the same as Labor and Delivery," she said. "Opposite wings."

The doors parted a moment later, and Sawyer stepped out with their son. "I should have been here with you. I didn't even know."

Emma sucked down a shaky breath as they moved along the brightly lit corridor toward the ICU. "It's okay," she promised, "because now you do."

Memories of waddling down that same hallway a few short months ago rushed back to her. Water broken, doubled over in pain. It was the most beautiful and terrifying night of Emma's life. Sara had been a total mess, completely freaked-out, running ahead of Emma to clear the path and waving her arms like she was hailing a taxi. They'd both been sure that Emma might deliver Henry at any moment. They'd read all the books and still knew nothing. It had been another twelve hours before Henry made his big debut. Emma slept more than Sara that night, thanks to the blessed epidural. Sara sat vigil, reading the tabloids and retelling funny stories from their childhood when Emma had woken. She'd held Emma's hand through every contraction, been the perfect coach, a dedicated aunt and a devoted sister.

And Emma wanted her back.

She gritted her teeth against the urge to cry. She'd already cried enough these last two days to fulfill her quota for a lifetime. Instead, she hiked her chin up an inch and approached the desk with resolve. "Hello, I'm Emma Hart. I'm here to see Kate Brisbane."

The nurse gave her and Sawyer a long look. "Are you family?"

"Yes," she lied

"Well, as I've explained to her other family members—" the nurse motioned to a waiting room full of people behind them "—Kate is still unconscious, and we're only allowing immediate family five-minute sessions. You can take a seat with your relatives, and when she's ready for another visitor, you can decide among yourselves who it will be."

Emma's cheeks warmed. She hadn't thought of all the real family members who might be there for Kate. "Thank you," she said, taking Sawyer's hand

and moving into the waiting room. "Well, that didn't go the way I wanted."

Sawyer gave her fingers a squeeze.

A dozen heads turned their way. She recognized one as Detective Rosen.

The detective stood and shook the hands of the couple he'd been speaking with, then came to meet Emma and Sawyer near the doorway. "I guess you saw the morning news."

Emma raised her eyebrows. "I guess so. Were you going to contact me if I hadn't?"

"We didn't see a reason to reach out to you just yet," the detective hedged. "We're looking into Kate's accident to determine if there's a connection."

Emma barked a humorless laugh. "*If* there's a connection? There's no way this was a coincidence," she said, crossing her arms over her chest. "This happened because Sara worked with Kate, and someone probably saw me talking with her yesterday."

The detective opened his arms and stepped forward, corralling them into the hallway, away from Kate's family. "We don't know that," he whispered.

"You do know that," she countered. "First, some psychopath walks right into my home and tears Sara away, then I'm attacked outside the credit union where she works. Our home is broken into that night, and this morning Sara's assistant manager is hit by a car. You don't have to have a signed confession to know these things are all part of a bigger picture."

Sawyer angled himself in on the detective, voice

low. "Have you at least matched the fingerprints or blood in Sara's room to someone yet?"

"No," Detective Rosen said flatly. "Those things take time, and as for the signed confession, it would be nice because I can't assume anything. The investigation must be based on facts for it to hold up in court, and we can't afford to play catch and release with murderers. They tend to not play nice upon release."

Emma pressed the heels of her hands to her eyes.

"What about you?" Detective Rosen asked. "Were you able to think of anything else that might help us catch whoever was in your home? Did you notice anything missing when you straightened up your sister's room?"

Emma shook her head and dropped her hands to her sides. "Not yet," she said, suddenly ashamed to admit she'd left the home right after he did. "Maybe they were looking for the notebook." She lifted her thumb to her mouth and bit into the skin along her thumbnail. "When will you hear back from your lab?"

"A few days to a couple weeks," he said, lifting a hand to stop her complaint before she had time to voice it. "Knox County doesn't have a lab. We have to send our work out, then it has to get in line behind the work of every other district in our situation." He pulled a phone from the inside pocket of his jacket. "Excuse me."

Emma frowned as the detective walked away. She

turned to Sawyer, frustration stinging her nose and throat. "Can you believe this?"

He headed back for the elevator. "Let's take another look at Sara's notebook. It's the only real lead we have, and it'll keep us busy. I've sent photos of the pages to my team at Fortress. Wyatt is good with puzzles like this. Maybe we can at least figure out if the notebook is relevant."

"Okay," she agreed. She'd nearly forgotten about the notebook with everything else going on. Maybe it was nothing, but if it was something that would bring Sara home, she needed to get copies to anyone who could help.

SAWYER MATCHED HIS pace to Emma's as they moved across the parking lot to his truck. She was clearly upset, and he understood why. Investigations didn't move as swiftly as they should, nothing like what was portrayed on television, and the truth was that finding Sara the old-fashioned way would be much quicker than waiting for feedback from a lab in the next county. Lucky for them, he had the men of Fortress Security at his disposal.

He beeped his truck doors unlocked, then secured a sleeping Henry inside. As much as Sawyer missed the kid's smiling face, he was glad someone could still rest. He certainly couldn't.

He slid behind the wheel, powered the windows down and waited while Emma buckled up. The warm autumn breeze fluttered her hair, sending her sweet scent over him. He gripped the wheel a little tighter in response.

"Why do you think someone tried to kill Kate?" Emma asked, gathering her hair over one shoulder.

"I don't know," he admitted. "Maybe she knew more than she let on when the two of you spoke."

Sawyer scanned the lot for signs of anyone who'd taken an interest in them. A man on a motorcycle in the next row caught his attention. His bike faced away from their truck, but he dropped his cigarette and ground it out with his boot when Sawyer started the engine.

Emma turned a guilty expression in Sawyer's direction. "Is it awful that this hit-and-run gives me hope for Sara?"

He settled back in his seat, watching to see what the motorcyclist did next. "How so?"

"Maybe the fact these horrible things keep happening is an indication that whoever took Sara is still trying to get all the evidence she has on him. I think he'll keep her alive until he's sure he's covered his tracks and collected everything against him. The night he took her, he kept asking who she'd told. 'Who did you tell? Who did you tell?'" Emma lowered her voice to something fairly menacing as she repeated the question. She rubbed her palms over the gooseflesh on her arms as she spoke. "And Kate's attack tells us something else. The man who took Sara has a partner or a team or something. You shot someone last night, and there was a lot of blood left

behind for a flesh wound. I can't imagine anyone
pulling off a hit-and-run only a few hours after taking a bullet like that." She looked over her shoulder
at the hospital. "So there are at least two men. The
one who took Sara and mugged me, and the guy who
broke in last night. Do you think Detective Rosen
thought to ask the hospital staff if anyone was admitted with a gunshot wound last night?"

"Yeah," Sawyer said, shifting into Drive as the motorcycle cruised out of the parking lot. "He would've
reached out to them right away, and even if he didn't,
hospitals have to report knife and gunshot wounds.
It's the law."

Emma settled back in her seat. "Right. Good."

Sawyer took the next left and headed in the opposite direction as the motorcycle. Something about
the man had put his instincts on edge, and there was
little Sawyer could do about it with Emma and Henry
in tow. For all he knew, the driver had intended to
get his attention and draw him down a certain path
where trouble awaited. On his own, Sawyer would
have loved the opportunity for engagement, but for
now, he needed to keep Emma and Henry safe.

"I can't stop wondering why someone would have
hit Kate," Emma said. "You were right when you
said she might've known more than she let on, but
in what way? Was she part of the scheme all along,
whatever it is? Did she become a loose end? Or did
Sara confide in Kate when she hadn't confided in
me? And why?"

"Maybe it wasn't like that," Sawyer suggested. "Maybe Sara stumbled across an issue at work and asked Kate about it. You said Kate told you Sara had questions. Maybe just knowing Sara's concerns was enough for the criminal to want to shut her up."

Emma pulled her lips to the side. "Maybe. I didn't ask her what Sara's questions were. I only asked how Sara had seemed the last few days, and Kate said Sara had been fine. Maybe a little tired, but she hadn't noticed anything significant or helpful."

Sawyer glanced her way. "Could she have been lying? If Sara had confided in her, then been abducted, it would make sense for her to hide what she knew. She could have reasoned that she would be taken too."

Emma bit into the skin along her thumbnail. "I should have asked her more questions."

Sawyer followed signs for the scenic byway. They could take the road through the national forest all the way back to his place without ever getting on the highway. The speed limits were much lower, but less traffic would make it easier to know if they were being followed.

His phone rang in his cup holder, and he recognized Wyatt's number immediately. He poked the speaker button to answer. "Hey," he said. "You've got me and Emma on speaker. We're in the truck headed back to the lake house now. What do you have?"

"Hey, Emma," Wyatt said, taking a minute to be

cordial. "I'm real sorry you and your sister are going through all this."

Her eyes glossed with instant tears. "Thank you."

"We'll get her back," he said. "I'm working on these numbers now, and Sawyer's a force to be reckoned with on search and rescue."

Sawyer's gut wrenched at his friend's high praise. Sawyer's last search and rescue mission had gotten his team killed. "What have you learned about the numbers?" he asked.

"They're accounts, like you said, locals attached to overseas partners, I think. I want to call your cousin, Blake, at the FBI on this. He can dig deeper than I can—legally anyway—if he takes an interest, and I think he will."

"Blake's card is on my desk. If you can't find it, call his brother West. He's the sheriff over in Cade County, Kentucky."

"On it," Wyatt said. "And, Emma…congratulations on the baby. Sawyer sent me some pictures. He's handsome as a derby stallion."

Emma smiled. "Thanks." She slid her eyes Sawyer's way. "You'll have to meet him someday."

"Plan to," Wyatt said. "I'll be in touch about these numbers."

Sawyer disconnected and turned his attention back to the road. "I sent a few pictures of Henry to the team when I sent the notebook scans."

Emma's smile grew. "Good."

The road through the national forest was wind-

ing and peaceful, a stark contrast to their lives. Lush
foliage on either side masked the brilliant blue sky
overhead, but shafts of determined sunlight filtered
between the leaves and branches to create a marvel-
ous display on the blacktop stretching uphill before
them. Sawyer had been to a lot of places around the
world, but there was no place more beautiful than
this. Tennessee had always had everything he needed.
At the moment, he thought, glancing through his cab,
he had everything he needed right there in his truck.

Henry fussed, and Emma twisted in her seat to
reassure him.

"Sawyer?" she said softly, turning forward as the
truck floated around another downhill curve. "Did
you notice the motorcycle at the hospital?"

"Yes," he said. "Why?" His gaze flicked to his
rearview mirror and found the answer. A black motorcycle with a rider in matching helmet and gear
blinked into view, then vanished behind the curve
of the mountain as the winding road carried them
steeply down.

"It's him, isn't it?" she asked.

Sawyer didn't answer. He couldn't be sure at that
distance, but his gut said it was the same man. "I'll let
him pass on the next straight stretch," he said. "We'll
get the number on the license plate and contact Detective Rosen." Even if the rider's reappearance was
nothing, it was worth a phone call to be sure.

Sawyer pressed the brake gently, reducing his

speed around the next sweeping curve. The pedal was softer than before, working, but not quite right.

The motorcycle drew nearer, its pint-size Alabama plate clearly visible now.

The road straightened before them, and Sawyer powered his window down, reaching an arm out and waving the man around as he continued to slow.

The motorcycle fell back.

"What's he doing?" Emma asked, voice quaking.

"I don't know." Sawyer stepped on the gas as they headed up the next hill. "Give Detective Rosen a call. Maybe they can run the plate. Tell him we'll get turned around and head over to the station. I don't like this."

Emma dug her phone from her pocket.

Sawyer crested the next hill and began the sharp decline on the other side. There was a wide lookout and parking lot with multiple trailheads at the base of the hill. It would be a good place to turn and head back before their tail figured out they were staying in the next county and not just out to enjoy the scenic drive. It would also give Sawyer a chance to look at his spongy brakes.

"That's right," Emma said, describing the situation into her phone. She unfastened her seat belt and turned onto her knees to stare through the back window. "Sawyer, slow down a little more. I can't read the numbers on his plate."

Sawyer added pressure to the pedal, and it slid easily down. Alarm shot through his system and a curse slipped between his lips. The brakes were out. The motorcycle wasn't tailing them. He was monitoring them. He'd probably cut the brake lines at the hospital and was watching to see the efforts pay off.

"Emma," he said, eyes widening as a huge camper trailer headed up the mountain in their direction, barely between the narrow curving lines. "Turn around." He hugged the mountain on his right, looking for a way to slow them down, even as the grade of the road seemed to steepen.

Henry gave a small cry in complaint, and Sawyer's heart constricted further. "Emma," he growled this time. "Turn around," he ordered. "Buckle up."

"I can almost read the plate," she said.

Sawyer took the next bend at nearly fifty miles per hour. The sign had suggested thirty-five.

Emma fell against the door, thrown off balance by the speed of the turn. "Slow down," she snapped, fumbling for her seat belt.

"I can't." Sawyer ground the words out. He adjusted his white-knuckle grip on the steering wheel and pressed the limp brake pedal into the floorboards. "My brakes are out."

"What? How?"

He pulled the shifter down from Drive, dropping it into a lower gear. The engine growled in protest. "I think someone punctured the line at the hospital. The brakes were fine when we left, but every time I've depressed the pedal since then, I've been pumping brake fluid onto the ground. Now we're out."

She covered her mouth with one hand, and Sawyer knew she understood what they were facing. She relayed the situation to Detective Rosen in sharp gasps, voice cracking and breaking on each desperate word.

The road plateaued slightly before taking another downward turn. Sawyer pulled the shifter again, moving it into the lowest gear. The engine revved and groaned, shooting the rpm gauge into the red.

Before them, a line of cars plugged away behind a slow-moving school bus. *Beep! Beep! Beep!* He jammed his thumb against his emergency flashers and continued a battering assault on his horn. Silently swearing and begging the drivers to get the message. His truck was out of control, and if they didn't move, he was going to take them all out with him.

The cars veered sharply, one by one, skidding into the soft shoulder against the hillside on the right as Sawyer's truck barreled past. A thick plume of dust lifted into the air as the vehicles skidded to a stop.

The school bus continued on.

Henry cried in the seat behind Sawyer, probably startled half to death by the blaring horn. His protests grew steadily more fervent as the truck closed in on the school bus. Tiny horrified faces came into view, staring back at him through the dusty emergency exit.

The road curved again, and the bus's brake lights came on.

Sawyer yanked the emergency brake and the

truck made a horrendous sound. Dark, acrid smoke clouded the air outside his window, filtering through his vents and causing Emma to cough, but the truck didn't stop.

With no other choice to make, Sawyer gritted his teeth and resolved to leave the road at any cost. Whatever he hit, short of a hiker, would be better than the bus full of children or careening over the mountainside. He held his position between the lines as he took the plunging curve around the mountain, seeking the first semilevel place to exit and slow his runaway vehicle.

At first sight of a trailhead around the bend, he pulled hard on the wheel. The truck slipped beside the school bus and over the rough, rocky berm with a deep guttural roar. The school bus swerved over the yellow line, and the pickup tore off-road completely, cutting a wild path through the miniature parking lot at the trailhead and taking a wooden sign with the location's official name down with it. The windshield cracked as the wood splintered and deflected off it.

Beside him, Emma threw her hands out as if the windshield might burst, and she screamed loud enough to chill Sawyer's blood.

Outside, people screamed and ran. They yanked babies from strollers and lifted children from the grass, launching their families against the tree-covered hillside. A mass of children in matching T-shirts fled a pavilion beyond the lot, and Sawyer directed his truck toward the newly emptied structure, hoping the slight uphill grade and a series of small collisions could safely slow the vehicle.

One by one, the picnic tables exploded under the impact of his truck's grille. One by one, the damage lessened until the little table and the hill brought his truck to a whiplashing stop.

In the parking lot behind them, a black motorcycle cruised calmly past.

Chapter Eight

Sawyer met the police and paramedics in the parking lot and directed them to where Emma and Henry sat on the grass. The path of destruction from the main road to the grassy bank opposite the pavilion was broad and littered with the fragments of state-donated picnic seating. Miraculously, no one had been killed, unless Sawyer counted the trailhead sign, row of picnic tables and his truck.

Detective Rosen joined them several minutes later, having stopped to speak with a number of witnesses and onlookers. "Are you all okay?" he asked, turning his eyes to the paramedic as he walked away.

"Yes, just shaken," Emma said, speaking for them all. "What did you learn?" She tipped her head to indicate the crowd behind them while Henry slept soundly in her arms.

"The Alabama plate was bogus," Detective Rosen said. "A bystander caught the motorcycle on video while taping your out-of-control truck. My guys ran the numbers, but that plate hasn't been in use in a decade. Probably thrown out and picked up by someone."

Sawyer lowered himself onto the grass beside Emma and looped a protective arm across her back.

She leaned against him, deflated, and said, "So even with a license plate number, a description of the vehicle and a hundred witnesses, we still don't know who did this?"

"Sadly, no."

Sawyer gave her a gentle squeeze. "What else do you know?"

"We know the truck's brakes were definitely tampered with," Detective Rosen said.

Emma huffed a disgusted sigh, then pushed onto her feet with Henry in her arms. "I need a minute," she said, walking away.

Sawyer raised a brow at the detective. He stood and dusted his palms against his pants. "You need to figure this out," he said. "Half those kids probably caught the whole thing on video with their cell phones."

"They did," Detective Rosen said, "and we'll review every frame, but the motorcyclist was in head-to-toe black. No one knows what he looks like under the gear, and we don't have a plate for the vehicle. We're doing what we can with what we have to work with, which isn't much."

"What about the hospital parking lot?" Sawyer asked. "My brakes were fine when I left. Then they got spongy and went out before I realized what was happening. The guy on the bike was there when we left. I think he might've punctured the lines while we were inside, so I wouldn't know what happened until it was too late. If you review the security feed from the cameras in that lot, you'll find him."

"We can try," he said, pulling a cell phone from his pocket. "But you should know the cameras outside the credit union, which would have been useful in identifying Emma's mugger or the hit-and-run driver, were out. I don't think it's a coincidence."

Sawyer tipped his head back and shut his eyes for a moment. "That's because it's not. These crimes were all planned. It's not good news for the police, or the victims."

"Mr. Lance?"

Sawyer opened his eyes. The tow truck operator lumbered in his direction. "Where do you want the truck taken?"

Sawyer eyeballed the extended cab of the logoed vehicle. "Wherever you recommend," he said. "Would you mind taking us to a local car rental company on the way?"

Two hours later Sawyer steered a rented SUV home from the police station, using the flattest and most low-trafficked route possible between counties. He'd rented the new vehicle under his company's name and given Fortress Security's address in case anyone tried to track him through the rental.

Sawyer's rustic A-frame house came into view through the trees, and he felt his shoulders relax.

He went straight to the kitchen for two glasses of ice water, and Emma curled onto the couch with Henry on her lap. She accepted the ice water with deep, thirsty gulps, but the fear and uncertainty in her eyes broke Sawyer's heart. He'd vowed to protect her and their son at all costs, but they'd nearly died at his hand today.

Sawyer brought up the photos of Sara's notebook on his phone as he made his way to the living room. He needed to put a name to their assailant before someone came at them again. He had a duty to protect Henry and Emma, *his son and his...* The thought twisted into a painful knot. Henry was his son, but Emma wasn't *his* anything anymore.

He hated that truth nearly as much as he hated the man who kept trying to hurt her.

Emma pulled her feet beneath her on the couch and turned wide blue eyes on Sawyer. "If the motorcyclist knew your truck, then he must know your name."

"Not necessarily," Sawyer said, determined to keep his cool.

"If he knows your name, he can find your address," she said. "He can find Henry."

Sawyer shook his head and offered her his hand. "It won't be easy," he said. "My truck, like my house, is registered to the company."

"But the company has a website," she said. "The website has a list of the Fortress team members' names. *Your name*," she said.

"I will protect you," he said. "This looks dire now, but it will be okay. I'm sure of it." And he intended to do anything he could to keep that promise.

The fire in Emma's eyes dimmed, and she shook her head in a look of resignation. "He'll find us again, Sawyer. He won't stop, and it's only a matter of time."

Sawyer took a seat at her side. He wanted to encourage and reassure her, but he was having trouble believing she was wrong. Instead, he held his phone between them, a photo from Sara's notebook on the screen. "Then we'd better find him before he finds us."

EMMA ANALYZED THE notebook pages late into the night, but nothing had changed. The numbers were still too long to be account numbers from Sara's credit union. Emma had already compared her fourteen-digit account number to the massive thirty-digit ones in the notebook. There was definitely more to the number-cluttered pages than just account numbers. She only wished she had a guess about what that might be.

Emma padded softly into the kitchen for another glass of water. Henry was fast asleep in his portable crib, and she'd already showered and changed into her favorite cotton shorts and tank top after dinner. If things went well for a change, Emma might get comfortable enough to fall asleep soon. The stress was taking a toll, and she needed the break. As it was, there was no way to release the ever-mounting tension, but a little rest could go a long way to taking the edge off, and that was what she needed most. She'd considered a jog along the lake earlier, or even a swim, but knowing a psychopath could pop up anywhere at any time had kept her close to her baby. Sadly, there would be no burning off steam for Emma until the nightmare was over. Assuming she survived at all.

The soft snick of an opening door put Emma's senses on alert. She stepped away from the countertop and leaned around the kitchen doorway for a look down the short hall. Scents of shampoo and body wash wafted out of the open bathroom door on a cloud of steamy air.

Emma's body tensed for new reasons as Sawyer moved into view. He pulled a black Fortress Security T-shirt over damp, rosy skin, still hot and beaded with water from the shower. His wet hair dripped over his temples and onto his broad, muscled shoulders.

She forced her mouth closed with effort.

"Sorry it took so long," he said, a look of profound guilt on his handsome face. "I was trying to decide if I should shave." He ran a broad palm over the dark two-day stubble, and Emma's knees went soft with an onslaught of memories. She'd intimately enjoyed Sawyer's stubble in the past. She knew firsthand about the rash it left on the tender flesh of her breasts and inner thighs when rubbed just right.

"I like the stubble," she said a bit breathlessly.

Sawyer's brows rose, and a sly grin slid over his handsome face. "That so?"

"Mmm-hmm." She cleared her throat and pressed a palm over her racing heart to calm the climbing beat.

Sawyer kept smiling.

"What?" she asked, pressing the glass of ice water to her lips before she lost control and kissed him again, the way she had the night before. *No*, she thought. She wouldn't kiss him like that again. That had been a chaste kiss on the cheek. Not even close to the way she longed to kiss or touch him. Emma swallowed hard and set the drink aside before she dropped it.

"You know," Sawyer began, closing in on her with intense brooding eyes, "we never really talked about the fact you kissed me last night."

Heat rose in her chest and cheeks at the reminder. Her gaze lingered on his lips. "It was a friendly, appropriate, completely innocent gesture," she said, hating the quaver in her voice.

"Why'd you do it?" he asked.

Emma struggled to swallow. Her chin hitched upward. "What do you mean?" She crossed her arms over her chest to protect her heart.

Sawyer took another step in her direction and reached for her, unfolding her arms and resting his broad palms against the curves of her waist. "Why'd you do it?" he asked again, widening his stance to plant one foot on either side of hers, pinning her against the countertop with his stare and the weight of his body.

Emma gripped his arms for balance, enjoying the heat and strength of him. "I missed kissing you," she whispered, unable to catch her breath. "I miss *you* and it makes it hard not to touch you."

Sawyer raised his hands slowly up her sides, grazing her ribs with his fingers, the sides of her breasts with his thumbs, then cradling her face between his palms, careful to avoid the darkening bruise along her cheek. "I missed you too," he whispered. The clean scents of toothpaste and mouthwash teased her senses for a heartbeat before Sawyer took her mouth with practiced skill.

He kissed her as perfectly as he had a thousand times before, and she curled herself around him in response. The taste of him on her lips pulled a greedy, exhilarating moan from her core, and she drank him in, enjoying the release much more than any evening jog.

She ignored the little voice in her head reminding her that a jog wouldn't break her heart when it was over.

Chapter Nine

Emma watched the sunrise over the lake, her legs draped over Sawyer's lap on his back-porch swing. They'd kissed until she was sure the burning need for more would turn her brain to ash, then she'd slipped away to gather her wits. The kiss had been enough for now, considering the excruciatingly complicated circumstances.

He'd found her on the porch swing, kissed her head and settled in at her side, pulling her legs over his and resting her feet on the cushion beside him.

"I think we should talk to the branch manager," she told Sawyer as the fiery sun finally lifted into the sky. "When I was at the credit union gathering the things from Sara's desk, Kate told me Sara had a bunch of questions for Mr. Harrison. Maybe her questions were related to whatever's going on here. Maybe he's part of this."

Sawyer stroked the backs of his fingers down her arm. "I'll give Detective Rosen a call."

"No." She pulled her legs away and planted her feet

on the floor. "We can call Detective Rosen afterward, especially if Mr. Harrison says anything useful, but I want to talk to him without the detective there. Besides, the police have already questioned the credit union staff. Maybe he'll be less on guard speaking to someone without a badge. He knows me, and maybe he knows something that can help me find Sara."

Sawyer frowned. "I understand why you want to go. I just wish you wouldn't."

Emma pursed her lips, prepared to fight as long and hard as necessary to get her way on this. "It wasn't a request for permission."

His lips quirked, apparently tempted to smile but thinking better of it. "Two women at that credit union have already been hurt. If it was up to me, I'd keep you in my pocket until the danger passed. Or book us a room at one of those all-inclusive resorts under assumed identities so we could sleep with both eyes closed for a night or two."

Emma's heart sputtered. "I can't leave Sara," she said. "I won't."

Sawyer tucked flyaway hair behind her ear. "I know. I was just enjoying a daydream where I know you're safe."

She smiled. "Then you'll take me to the credit union when it opens?"

He tipped his head over one shoulder and released a heavy sigh. "The manager is a significant link between Kate and Sara, so it's worth a conversation. I just don't know if it's a good idea to cross his path.

Like you said, he might know something, or he might be the one behind all this."

"That's exactly why we need to talk to him."

TRAFFIC WAS LIGHT on the way to the credit union. At nine fifteen, the school buses had already delivered the students, most office workers were at their desks and lunch hour was another two hours away. Sawyer parked the rented SUV across the street at the end of the block, and went to join Emma on her side of the vehicle.

Henry was bright-eyed and smiling as she tucked him snugly into a thick circle of fabric hung over one shoulder and across her body. He looked like a purse with a pacifier, and it made Sawyer smile.

"Are you sure you don't need to hold on to him?" he asked.

Emma shot him a sharp look.

He raised his palms

A few moments later he opened the credit union door for her, still eyeballing the strange circle of fabric. "Will that thing fit me?"

"I doubt it," she said. "A lady at church measured me for it, but Henry's also got a backpack he enjoys. That's one size fits all."

"You put him in a backpack?" Sawyer frowned. "Whatever happened to just carrying your kid?"

"Baby slings and backpacks keep your hands free," she answered softly. "Not everyone has someone to

help carry the baby *and* haul their groceries or un-
lock the car door or pay the cashier."

The words tightened Sawyer's core. Emma had
needed help with those things, and help hadn't been
there. *He* hadn't been there.

"Emma," a maternal voice cooed. A woman with
a round face and salt-and-pepper hair motioned them
to the transaction counter. "Come on over here and
let me see that little man," she said.

Emma obliged with a smile. "How are you, Gladys?"

"Better than you, it seems." She frowned at the
angry bruise on Emma's pretty face. "I heard about
your mugging, the break-in. Sara, then poor Kate.
It's a darn shame. Things are all but sideways around
here lately. If there's anything I can do to help you,
just ask. I can cook, clean, babysit. Whatever you
need. I've already been praying night and day."

"Thank you," Emma said, wrapping her arms
around Henry, something Sawyer had noticed her
doing anytime she looked uneasy or afraid.

Henry kicked and stretched, discontent at standing still, Sawyer suspected.

"Here." Sawyer reached for his son. "I can take
him. You can visit."

Gladys watched, wide-eyed, as Emma passed the
baby to him. "Well, now I think you've forgotten to
introduce me to someone important here. You never
let anyone hold that baby."

Sawyer gathered his son high on his chest and
kissed his cheeks.

"Gladys," Emma said, "this is Sawyer Lance."

Gladys sucked air. "The daddy."

Sawyer extended a hand in her direction. "Yes, ma'am."

Her smile grew as they shook. "I've been praying for you too," she said. "These two have needed you something fierce."

"I've needed them too," he said, releasing Gladys's hand and pulling Emma against his side.

Gladys pressed her hands to her chest.

An elderly couple came to stand in line behind Sawyer.

"Well," Emma said, "we'd better get out of your way so you can work. Is Mr. Harrison in his office?"

Gladys dipped her head and lowered her voice. "No. He didn't come in today, and as far as I know he didn't call off. Instead, we've got that one." She pointed to the office where a vaguely familiar face sat behind the desk, staring at the computer. "His name is Christopher something or other from our corporate office."

Sawyer moved out of the way, and Emma followed.

"Thank you," Emma told Gladys before turning her back to the woman and trapping Sawyer in her sharp gaze. "Why do you think Mr. Harrison isn't here?" she asked. "And where do you think he is?"

Those were very good questions. "Let's see if Christopher from corporate knows," he suggested.

The tall blond man at the manager's desk stood when he noticed their approach. He met them outside the office and pulled the door shut behind him. "Good morning," he said. "What can I do for such a fine-looking family this morning?" His name tag proclaimed the words *Christopher Lawson*, and his clothes said he knew how to pick them. All quality, neat as a pin and fashionable down to his tassel-topped loafers.

Emma offered him a polite smile. "We were just looking for Mr. Harrison," she said. "We always say hello when we're in the neighborhood."

Christopher crossed long arms over a narrow chest and widened his lanky stance. "Well, I'm happy to pass the message on, but Mr. Harrison's not in today."

"Shame," Emma said, dropping the smile. "Is he ill?"

Christopher shrugged, curious blue eyes twinkling. "Hard to say. Is there anything I can help you with?"

"No." Emma slid her hand into Sawyer's. "I guess we'll have to stop back the next time we're in the area." She swung Sawyer toward the door and nearly dragged him outside.

They crossed the street at the corner before speaking. Sawyer repositioned Henry in his arms and unlocked the SUV doors. "What do you think?" he asked. "Is Mr. Harrison sick or halfway to Aruba?"

Emma frowned. "Maybe, but if he's the one who took Sara and he's leaving the country, then what happens to my sister?"

Sawyer didn't want to answer that. He buckled Henry into his car seat, then went around to climb behind the wheel. "What did you think of Christopher?"

"I don't know," she said. "He was strangely familiar, but I don't think we'd ever met, if that makes any sense."

Sawyer buckled up and checked his mirrors before pulling into traffic. "Any idea where Mr. Harrison lives? Maybe the best way to find out why he's not at work is to ask him ourselves."

Emma tapped the screen of her phone. "I might have his address," she said. "The office Christmas party was at his house a couple years ago, and the invitation was digital." She paused to look at Sawyer. "Maybe that's how I recognize Christopher. There were a few folks from corporate at the party."

"Which way?" Sawyer asked.

Emma called out the turns through town as Sawyer manned the wheel. Thirty minutes later they arrived at an upscale parklike neighborhood, befitting a middle-aged banker. "I think his house is the brick one-story at the end of the road," she said. "I remember parking in the back. There's a big concrete area outside a giant garage and a pool."

"Here?" Sawyer asked as they motored slowly toward the brick home. A cluster of people stood on the sidewalk across the street as Sawyer turned the corner toward the rear parking area Emma had described. Emergency vehicles came into view.

"What on earth?" Emma sat forward. "That's Detective Rosen's car. Do you think the manager has been keeping Sara here all along? Could they have found her? Why wouldn't the police have contacted me?"

Sawyer shifted into Park, and Emma leaped out. He unfastened a sleeping Henry from the seat behind his and took his time following Emma through the crowd.

A pair of older women smiled at Henry, and Sawyer slowed to let them admire the baby.

"Hello," he said cordially. "Do you have any idea what's going on here? We were just on our way over for a visit."

"Oh, dear," the woman on the right said softly. "I'm so sorry."

Sawyer raised his brows. "About?"

"I was walking Mr. Bootsy after breakfast, and I heard a terrible calamity coming from inside the house," she said. "I didn't want to seem as if I was being nosy, so we crossed the street, but then there was a loud blast, like a gunshot. I ran right home and called the police after that."

"Sawyer." Emma's voice turned his head in her direction. The horror in her eyes set his feet into a jog.

Beside her, a pair of EMTs guided a gurney toward the home, a folded body bag on top.

Chapter Ten

Sawyer cut through the crowd to Emma's side. He wrapped his arm around her and pulled her against his chest, practically reading her mind. "The bag's not for Sara," he said, leaning his mouth to Emma's ear. "It's most likely for Mr. Harrison."

Emma swallowed hard as she looked up at him, her breaths coming far too shallowly. She looked to Henry, and Sawyer passed the baby into her arms. Emma snuggled him to her chest and nuzzled him tenderly. Her gaze trailed the gurney with the body bag on its path to the house. "How can you be sure?"

Sawyer took Emma's trembling hand. "Come on," he said, giving her fingers a tug. He pulled her away from the crowd and through the front yard instead. "Neighbors heard a commotion this morning." He caught Emma's eye as they approached Mr. Harrison's porch. Sawyer climbed the steps, silently towing Emma along with him. "My guess is that Mr. Harrison figured out what Sara was onto with all those questions before her abduction, and he asked the wrong person about it. That or the man who took her found out she'd taken her concerns to Mr. Harrison. Either way, I'm sure he was the fatality here."

"We don't know he's dead," Emma said.

Sawyer tipped his head briefly to each shoulder. "This is his house, and we saw the body bag."

Emma sighed. "We should talk to Detective Rosen."

Sawyer peered through one of the front windows before moving onto the next. "I'm looking for him." He tried the door and a second window, then went back down the steps and around the opposite side of the house with Emma in his wake.

A row of flowering trees and bushes cast long shadows over the side yard, making their movement across the lawn less noticeable to traffic and onlookers. "Here," he whispered, motioning her closer. "Listen."

The curtains were drawn on the next window, but a number of male voices warbled inside. Sawyer adjusted his position for a look through the slight part in heavy linen panels. From his new vantage, he could see the reason for the crowd and emergency responders as well as the body bag.

Mr. Harrison was splayed over a desk in what appeared to be a home office, a handgun near his limp hand and a bullet wound at his temple.

Sawyer stepped back to make room for Emma, who slid into the small space before him.

She rose to her toes to see above the sill, then fell back with a gasp. "He killed himself," she whispered. "Why would he do that?"

Sawyer braced his palms on her waist, steadying her, then took her hand and finished the circle around Mr. Harrison's home. They crossed the small courtyard by the swimming pool and emergency vehicles, and let themselves into the kitchen.

Detective Rosen stood inside, rubbing his chin with one hand and speaking quietly to an EMT. He started at Sawyer and Emma's appearance. "What are you doing here?" he asked, skipping the pleasantries.

"Door was open," Sawyer said. "What about you?" He moved farther into the room, getting a better look at the crime scene. It took only a minute to know his gut was right. Mr. Harrison hadn't committed suicide.

The detective frowned. "I'm a cop. I belong here. It's your appearance I'm concerned about."

Emma moved between them, positioning her back to the open office door where Mr. Harrison lay. "We were at the credit union this morning, and the man taking Mr. Harrison's place said he hadn't shown up or called off today."

"So you rushed right over?" the detective asked dryly.

Emma swallowed long and loud. "I thought his absence might have something to do with Sara's disappearance."

"Murder would also explain his failure to call off or show up," Sawyer said.

Detective Rosen lifted his brow. "Murder?"

Sawyer stepped forward. "That's why you're here,

isn't it?" He turned to face the office. "First responders probably noticed the angle of the wound is wrong for a suicide. Whoever held the gun before leaving it on the desk beside the victim's hand was standing over him. Mr. Harrison was shot at close range, but there are no muzzle burns around the wound. Most suicide victims press the barrel to their skin to ensure they get the job done." Sawyer had seen it firsthand, and more often than he cared to recall during his time in service. "Furthermore, the gun is beside his right hand, but his desk phone, mouse, pens and coffee mug are on his left, suggesting Mr. Harrison was left-handed."

Detective Rosen sucked his teeth but didn't argue. "There are no signs of forced entry," he said, casting a look at the kitchen door, where Emma stood with Henry, looking more than ready to leave.

Sawyer nodded. He'd noticed that too. "He knew the killer, or he had another reason to open the door to him. Someone posing as a utility worker, salesman, new neighbor…looking for a lost dog, could've been anything."

Detective Rosen rubbed his chin again. "The crime scene team is coming to check for prints." He opened his arms the way he had at the hospital and stepped toward the door, herding Sawyer back to Emma, then outside.

"Wait," Emma said, stepping out into the sun. "Could Sara have been here?"

"No." Detective Rosen shook his head. "There are no signs that anyone other than Mr. Harrison had been living here. Now, kindly remove yourselves from the property. Civilians aren't permitted at a crime scene."

EMMA'S SKIN CRAWLED with tension and grief as they moved away from the home. Back through the shaded yard and past the window where she'd seen Mr. Harrison's body. The image of him slumped over his desk would never be completely erased from her mind.

"Hey." Sawyer's palm found the small of her back.

A thick bout of nausea and panic rose through her core to her throat. "Take Henry," she said, fighting the terrible sensation and passing the baby to his father.

Sawyer pulled Henry to his chest, and Emma bent forward at the waist, huffing for air and hoping not to be sick on Mr. Harrison's lawn. She counted slowly, forcing her lungs to take bigger and deeper gulps of air despite the burn in her constricted throat with each pull.

Sawyer leaned her against him and rubbed her back. "It's okay. Take your time."

A few moments later her knees were weak, but the black dots in her vision had cleared. She straightened her spine and squared her shoulders with feeble resolve. "Sorry."

"Don't be," Sawyer said.

Emma pursed her lips. A thousand horrific thoughts cluttered her frightened mind. "What if we find Sara like that soon?"

"No," he said. "Sara's smart. She's cautious, and she's a fighter. I'm sure that whoever has her is no competition for her will to get back to you. We just have to figure out where she is."

Emma hoped he was right. Sara was strong, but maybe her captor was stronger. Maybe her physical injuries had weakened her mental ability to stay focused and fight. "I've been praying that she'll escape," Emma said, stepping back into the sunlight of the front yard, "but she was in bad shape. You should've seen the blood on our living room floor. The way he choked her and climbed on her. The sound when he hit her." Emma's teeth began to chatter despite the morning's heat.

Sawyer helped her into the SUV and fastened her seat belt for her before shutting the door.

She watched as he did the same for Henry, then climbed behind the wheel.

"What?" he asked, reaching for the ignition and checking his mirrors.

Emma unbuckled and slid across the bench to him. She pulled herself against his side and buried her face in the warm curve of his neck. She gripped the strong muscles of his shoulder and breathed him in until her racing heartbeat slowed to the steady confident pace of his. "This lunatic hit Kate with a car and shot Mr. Harrison. What's he going to do to Sara?"

Sawyer pulled her onto his lap and cradled her in his arms, sliding the seat back gently to make room.

"Sara's going to be okay," he whispered into her hair, "and so are you."

It had been a long time since Emma let someone else carry her burdens for her. Not since losing her parents had she truly let her guard down, and even then she shared the pain with Sara. Sitting there now, curled in Sawyer's arms made her dream of a life where she could trade off the work of being strong from time to time. Sawyer had been gone for a year, but he was back now. He was there with her and Henry, and maybe she couldn't make him stay, but she could make sure he knew that was what she wanted. That her heart had been torn open all over again at the sight of him, and only his enduring presence would heal her.

Sawyer's rough palm brushed the soft skin of her cheek. He tucked strong fingers beneath her chin and searched her face with soulful blue eyes. "What are you thinking?"

"I don't know what I'd do without you," she whispered.

Sawyer lowered his mouth to hers and kissed her gently before resting his cheek against the top of her head. "I hope you'll never again find out."

Emma agreed, and tonight she'd make sure Sawyer understood just how much she wanted him to stay.

Chapter Eleven

Sawyer held Emma's hand as they drove back through town. He stroked her fingers with the pad of his thumb and imagined a life where the three of them—Emma, Henry and himself—could spend days together doing whatever they wanted and getting to know one another, not haunting crime scenes in search of stolen loved ones and debating murder versus suicide. He struggled to keep his eyes on the road and off the people inside the SUV. He needed to protect them at all costs and find Emma's sister, but he wasn't sure what to do next. His team members were on other assignments, and already working the numbers from Sara's notebook in their spare time. Sawyer was supposed to be the man on call. The extra hands. But he'd gotten this call, and everything had changed. His jaw tightened and his grip on the wheel intensified. Keeping Emma and Henry safe made it impossible to go out on his own, and while there were some situations where a young family moved inconspicuously, the places he wanted to go would be dangerous for him alone, and he refused to be the reason Emma was ever frightened again.

If it was up to him, Sawyer would lock up Emma and Henry safely somewhere, maybe even back at Fortress Security with a few armed and trained bodyguards, then Sawyer would return to Emma's town. He'd start at the local pool halls and bars, asking anyone who'd had enough alcohol to loosen their lips if they'd heard about the missing woman or the hit-and-run. Surely in a community as small as Emma's all the thugs and lowlifes knew one another. Someone had surely bragged about the money they were going to come into. Someone would buy one too many rounds on him. There was jealousy among thieves, and Sawyer was sure he could find a lead the police couldn't if only he could divide himself in two to get to it. He gave Emma another long look, then glanced at Henry's sleeping face in the rearview mirror. They weren't officially his family yet, but he was willing to do anything in his power to make it that way, if Emma would have him.

She turned to face him at the stoplight, as if she'd somehow heard her name in his mind. "Can we stop at my place before we go back to yours?" she asked. "I'd like to pack some more of my things and what's left of Henry's. Maybe even bring his crib." The words were music to Sawyer's ears, but he hated the uncertainty he heard in them. Had he given her some reason to think he wouldn't be thrilled at the suggestion? Had their late-night make-out session not conveyed the fact that he wanted nothing more than to be with her, and with Henry, every day?

She watched him with an uplifted brow.

"All right," he said finally, simply. But he needed to do better. He needed to make his intentions crystal clear so there would be no room for misunderstanding. *Sooner rather than later*, he thought, *before anything else can go wrong.* There were already enough complications between them. "Why don't we stop by the outlets and buy a crib for my place?" Sawyer suggested. "There's no sense in hauling one back and forth when I need one now too."

"What?" Her narrow brows hunkered low between her eyes. "Why?"

"I want to spend as much time with Henry as possible now that I know he exists. It makes sense for him to have a room at my place too."

Emma's expression went flat, and she turned forward once more. "Okay."

"What?" Sawyer asked, taking the next right toward Emma's home. Clearly they weren't going shopping.

She bit into the skin along her thumbnail. "Nothing, it's fine."

Sawyer gave a dark chuckle. He hadn't been gone nearly long enough to have forgotten what *fine* meant. It meant she was mad, and for no good reason as far as he could tell.

She made a little fist and tucked her bitten thumb inside it, still forcing her attention outside as they took the final turn onto her long rural street.

He worked his jaw, determined to let her be mad about nothing. Except, she shouldn't be mad. She should be glad he wanted to be with his son as much as possible. Shouldn't she? Wasn't that the good, honorable and *right* thing to want? He squinted across the seat at her. "What's wrong?"

"Nothing."

Sawyer cut the engine in her driveway and turned toward her, throwing one arm over the seat back beside him. "Nope."

Emma's cheeks reddened. "Yep," she said, sliding out onto the gravel and shutting the door behind her. Hard.

Sawyer climbed out and met her at Henry's door, where she unlatched his car seat from the base. He considered taking the heavy carrier from her or at least offering to carry it, but Emma was upset, and he'd learned quickly that she kept Henry close at times like these. *Even if she was mad about nothing.*

He followed them to the front door and outstretched a hand, offering to hold the carrier while she dug for her key.

She hooked the seat in the crook of her arm and handled everything herself. A moment later she pointed her key at the lock and froze. She backed up a step and looked at Sawyer. "It's unlocked."

The frustration he'd felt toward her unexplained attitude bled away, and every instinct he had steeled him to defend her. He motioned Emma behind him as he turned the knob. She hurriedly obeyed.

The door swung easily inward, and Sawyer cursed. She was right. Someone had been there, and the house screamed with the evidence. He pulled his weapon and reached for Emma with his free hand, pulling her and Henry close behind him.

The house was in utter disarray. Every item in sight had been turned upside down. Someone was desperate to find something. *The thing that he had broken into Sara's room to find,* Sawyer thought. A good sign that whatever Sara had on this guy was still in play. A good sign because her life likely depended on that.

Sawyer ached to prowl through the upended room and shoot today's intruder the way he'd shot the last, but his legs locked and his muscles froze before he reached the center of the living room. He couldn't take his family one step farther into a potential ambush, and he couldn't send them out of his sight to wait. He stepped back, urging Emma onto the porch, then rushing her down the steps beside him to the SUV, where he locked them all inside and started the engine in case they needed to make a fast retreat.

His muscles ached to pounce on the man who'd done this, but that would have to wait. Right now, he had his family to think of.

THE POLICE ARRIVED within minutes of Emma's call to Detective Rosen. He came later, having been caught up at Mr. Harrison's murder scene. Comparatively, she supposed Mr. Harrison's situation had probably seemed more pressing, but she disagreed. She and Henry were still alive, still in danger, and finding out who kept coming at them seemed paramount to finding out who'd killed a man after the fact. Maybe if the police got to the bottom of her situation now, she and Henry would never end up like... Emma's stomach coiled at the thought of Mr. Harrison's fate becoming Henry's.

Emma took Henry to the rocker in the living room as men and women in uniforms began showing up in pairs. It was both profoundly tragic and strangely reassuring that the faces were becoming familiar to her. She'd seen them all at least once these last few days, some after Sara's abduction, others after her own mugging, the first break-in or the runaway truck scenario. The small-town police force was only so big, and now she'd met them all, or at least it seemed that way. Thankfully, they all knew that this was part of a complex ongoing investigation, and Emma hadn't had to repeat any information for them. She wasn't sure she could without bringing on an emotional breakdown, and there was no time for that.

She kept Henry close, singing softly and stroking his hair and cheek until he grew tired of watching the crowd and he dozed in her arms. Henry was her life now, and keeping him close to her heart seemed to be the only thing keeping her from losing her mind. As long as Henry was safe, everything else would be too.

Even if her mother's dishes were shattered and the bookshelves her father had made her on her tenth birthday were ruined. Even if every sweet memory she'd made before her parents' deaths were slowly being chipped away and ruined by one murderous psychopath…

If Henry was okay, Emma would be okay too.

Emma tried not to think about the scene before her. She didn't let her gaze or mind settle on the woman dusting her door for prints or the photographer snapping shots of her destroyed things. They were just *things*. But her stomach clenched at the sight of her framed photos scattered on the ground, some torn from the frames. Photos of her parents. Photos of Henry. Images of her and Sara through the years. How could she go on in a life without Sara? Emma wasn't even sure who she was without her for context. They were best friends. Confidantes. *Sisters*.

Sawyer walked into the room, instantly pulling her jangled nerves together. Something about his presence had a way of doing that. Calming her. He'd stuck to Detective Rosen's side after his arrival, talking, listening and occasionally making calls. She admired Sawyer's unwavering confidence under fire. Ironically, of all the terrible things they'd encountered together these last few days, she'd seen him rattled only once, and that was in the SUV earlier when he'd offered to buy a second crib for Henry and she'd abandoned the conversation.

Her spine stiffened with the memory. He wanted to get his own crib for Henry instead of sharing the crib she already had. *What's wrong?* he'd asked. Was he kidding? Only the fact that it had been the worst way possible for him to say he had no intentions of making a life with her. What he'd suggested sounded like the behavior of divorced couples, not reunited lovers making a fresh start. She didn't want two of everything or to split her son down the middle, raising him separately but together. She didn't want to be a separated couple who'd never even had the chance to be together.

Her heart rate sped with fresh frustration. She supposed she should be happy Sawyer wanted to be with Henry as much as possible, but given the fact she'd just decided to tell him how badly she wanted to build a life with him, the notion of a second crib had been an unexpected punch to her gut. She shook it off. Sawyer didn't know about her plans. It wasn't fair to be upset when he had no idea why. And, she reminded herself, after she told him what she wanted, there was no guarantee that he'd want it too. She'd have no right to be mad about that either. She let her eyes close briefly. She needed to prepare herself for that possibility.

For now, she owed him an apology and an explanation for her earlier behavior. He'd been nothing but kind and comforting to her despite his own feelings about getting the surprise of a lifetime when she'd introduced him to Henry. Of course, she wasn't in the mood to give an apology or an explanation, and both would have to wait until the house was straightened and empty of police officials. Until then, she rocked and sang and hoped Sara would be home soon. She *needed* her to be home soon.

Eventually, Sawyer walked the last of the cops onto the porch, and Emma rolled Henry's crib into the living room, then laid him in it. She wasn't ready to let him out of her sight, and she couldn't leave him anywhere there was a bullet hole in the wall beside his head.

Emma started a fresh pot of coffee and collected her cleaning supplies from where they'd been thrown out of the hall closet. As if Sara had kept her biggest secrets at the bottom of a can of Comet. Emma started by putting her living room back in order and giving everything a good scrub so Henry wouldn't be surrounded by chaos when he woke. She folded afghans and arranged throw pillows, straightened the curtains and lined books, quietly, back onto the built-in shelves along the fireplace. She shimmied the furniture back into the correct positions and righted the overturned vase, which had blessedly not broken in the spill. Goose bumps rose on her arms as she sprayed the cleanser on every flat surface and pretended that with enough elbow grease, she could rub all traces of the intruder's grubby hands off her and Sara's lives.

Sawyer returned as she put the last cleansing touch on her living room. "Nice," he said, looking wholly impressed.

"Thanks. One room down, eight more to go." She puffed air into overgrown bangs, then tucked them behind her ear. "What did Detective Rosen say?"

"He thinks whoever did this was looking for the notebook we gave him."

Emma agreed. She moved into the kitchen and put her table and chairs back in place, thankful for the work to busy her hands and give her restless nerves an outlet. "Did you talk to your team? Have they made any more progress with the pages you sent them?" She'd seen him on the phone and hoped that was the case.

"Wyatt's working on it." Sawyer restocked the pantry with fallen cans and boxes, then lifted the broom into his hands and worked it over the linoleum floor. He stilled when his phone rang. "It's Wyatt," he said, looking at the small screen. He set the cell phone on the counter and pressed the speaker button. "You're on speaker. I'm with Emma. What do you have?"

"Hey," Wyatt began, skipping the niceties this time and getting right down to business. "We were able to make a definitive match on all the numbers in Sara's notebook. The first account number represents an account at the Knox Ridge Credit Union, more than one hundred of them, actually. The back half of each number is a second account, as suspected, coordinating with a bank in the Cayman Islands. That's why the numbers all end the same way. Sara began each line with a transaction date, which accounts for the initial set of numbers on each line."

Emma wiped large wet circles over her countertop, trying to channel the excess energy while she processed the information. "Was Sara tracking an embezzlement scheme?"

"Maybe," Wyatt said. "Blake's looking into it further than I can, but that's the direction we're leaning."

Sawyer crossed his arms. "Could be money laundering. Could be both."

The phone was silent for a long beat before Wyatt simply added, "Yep."

Emma shivered as the implication settled in. "This is a lot bigger than I thought," she said, her mouth going dry with anxiety. "I thought Sara caught one guy doing something big enough to get him arrested. Now I know she caught someone stealing from at least a hundred people? Funneling funds offshore? And the man behind it is so unstable he'd kill to cover his tracks." She swallowed the painful mound of emotions piled in her throat and wrapped her arms around her unsettled stomach. "He killed Mr. Harrison. He tried to kill Kate. And us too." She swept her gaze from the phone to Sawyer and saw the truth in his eyes.

Whoever was doing these things would do whatever it took to be sure his stolen funds were safe.

Even murder a pair of sisters and a little baby.

Chapter Twelve

Sawyer worked at Emma's side for hours, enjoying the steady pace and easy partnership they'd fallen into midway through the kitchen cleanup. He scrubbed. She tidied. They were an excellent team. Emma knew where everything went. She knew how things worked. He, on the other hand, was decent with a scrub brush and lifted fallen items with less trouble.

Emma adjusted the volume on her phone dock's speaker as a new song began. She watched as he emptied another dustpan of broken glass into the trash bin. "I know I've said it before, but thank you, Sawyer," she said. "For helping me with this mess. For being here when we need you most."

Sawyer let the smile budding on his lips break free. "Where else would I be?" he asked with a wink. He watched as her own smile bloomed in return, and some of the day's horrendous weight lifted.

Working beside her, even at a task as unfortunate as theirs, reminded him of how good they were together. Emma was his perfect teammate. The yin to his yang. He'd never experienced anything like it, not even with his brothers in arms after years of fighting side by side. With Emma, it was different. Seamless. Better.

She stretched to set a pile of freshly folded jeans on her closet shelf, and Sawyer had to force his gaze back on the floor and dustpan.

There were perks to their camaraderie besides companionship. He also enjoyed her taste in music, and the playlist she'd started to help pass the time was filled with his favorites. A few of the selections were deeply nostalgic, and most of those memories included her.

Another bonus was the conversation. She didn't push or prod for more when he answered her questions, and she always answered his with depth and sincerity. She took her time, and he appreciated that.

The other benefit to their evening was watching her dead-sexy body bend and stretch for hours, a little sweat beading in the most deliciously distracting places.

Sawyer met her at the closet doors and placed the next few stacks of clothing on the shelves just above her head. "I've got it. Move over, shorty."

She bumped him with her hip. "I could have done that," she said, grinning. "I've been short all my life, you know. I've learned to get creative."

"No need to get creative when you've got an extra set of hands," he said.

"And they are *very* nice hands." Emma flashed a

wicked grin but didn't say another word as she went to refill her drawers with freshly washed and folded clothing. Whatever she'd been upset about in the SUV seemed to have passed. He planned to circle back to that subject later, when the work was done, but for now, he was just glad to see her smiling.

He didn't hate seeing her in her "work clothes" either. A few hours ago when she'd announced that she would change to finish cleaning, he'd expected her to return in oversize sweatpants or a holey T-shirt. Instead, she'd emerged from her room in a pair of short black running shorts and a fitted V-neck T-shirt. He could understand why the outfit worked for her. It couldn't possibly be hot or cumbersome, two definite benefits with so much bending, stretching and sweating ahead. Her outfit worked for him too, but all his reasons were currently testing his integrity and willpower.

Emma finished refolding the rest of her clothing and reloading the dresser drawers, then wiped a line of sweat off her brow. "I think that's it," she said. The hem of her shirt rose above the waist of her little shorts as she reached to peel the elastic band out of her hair and free her ponytail. The strip of exposed skin drew his attention to her middle, and his fingers curled at the sight of her creamy skin. Determined not to touch the gentle sway of her stomach or curves of her waist, he braced his hands on his hips. Emma wasn't his to touch that way anymore. And this was hardly the right time to address the possibilities that she might reconsider him for the job anytime soon.

He dragged his gaze to hers. "I guess our work is done here."

She smiled, and he knew he'd been caught ogling, but was that all? Could she see the shameless truth in his expression? That he wanted her in every possible way, even if this was a terrible time to want more than to keep her safe and bring her sister home?

"What now?" he asked, intentionally leaving the question open to interpretation.

"Now," she said, plucking the thin cotton fabric of her white T-shirt away from her sweat-dampened skin, "I need a shower." She shook out her hair and gave him the sexiest damn smile he'd ever seen before walking away. "I won't be long," she said, moving in the direction of her en suite bath. She hooked a finger at him as she crossed the threshold.

Sawyer swallowed a low groan and went after her.

A small, distant cry pulled him up short. He caught the doorjamb in both palms and dropped his head forward in disappointment, but only for a moment. He lifted a genuine smile to Emma's stunned, maybe even disappointed eyes. "Duty calls," he said, smile growing.

"Daddy duty," she said, smiling back.

He liked the sound of that. He turned on his heel and gave her one last look over his shoulder. "I'm going to have to insist on a rain check for that shower."

Emma laughed. "If you handle daddy duty so I can soak this day off right now, you've got more than a shower coming your way."

Sawyer gave a low wolf whistle on his way back to Henry's crib in the living room, where he would soon get to hold the other love of his life for a while.

EMMA TOOK HER time in the shower, both soaping up and winding down. She let herself imagine Sawyer had joined her under the steamy spray, and a wave of similar memories pummeled through her. Emma's time with Sawyer, before Henry, had always been intense. He'd asked for her number the moment they'd met and called the same night, before she'd made it back to her car. He'd told her he didn't have much time. That he was a soldier on leave for thirty days, and he planned to make the most of his time. When he asked her out, the sound of her name on his tongue had felt like coming home. Maybe that was what people meant when they said "love at first sight." Whatever it was, being with him again had brought it all back in a powerful rush.

She spent a few more minutes enjoying the fantasy that she wasn't alone before stepping out of the shower and pulling herself back together. Thoroughly dried and relaxed, she paired a jean skirt and short-sleeved button-down with bare feet in sneakers, then blew out her hair until it was soft on her shoulders. A little lip gloss and mascara, and Emma was ready to face the rest of her night, whatever that might hold.

Sawyer's voice rumbled down the hall from the kitchen as she stepped into the hall. She followed the sounds of his singing until she reached the kitchen, where he two-stepped Henry through the room.

Henry looked tiny in Sawyer's muscled arms, his narrow body stretched against Sawyer's broad chest. Their matching blue eyes lit with each buoyant step. Just when she'd been certain Sawyer Lance couldn't get any more desirable, this happened. It wasn't fair. Seeing him like this with their son was more than she'd ever dared to dream for, and here he was, instantly devoted and obviously happy. It was exactly the way she'd felt the moment she'd realized she was pregnant.

She and Sawyer had created the most precious gift imaginable together, and the beauty of that truth tugged at her heart. Despite everything else going wrong in her life at the moment, her heart overflowed with gratitude.

Sawyer raised a smile in her direction as the song ended. His jaw went slack before his lips broke into a wide smile. "You must be going somewhere special looking like that."

"I am," she said. "I've got a whole night planned at the lake with two very important men."

"Two, huh?" Sawyer strode to meet her in the room's center, turning Henry so he could watch the approach. "Sounds like some lucky guys."

Emma pulled Henry into her arms and kissed his cheek. "I'm the lucky one," she said. And it was true. She hated knowing it would end soon. That Sawyer would go back to his new life in progress, and she'd only see him during the drop-offs and pickups when they traded Henry like a shared book or CD.

Sawyer planted a kiss on Henry's head. "What do you say we get out of here?" he asked. "The house is spotless. The work is done. Let's head back to the lake house. I think it's my turn for a shower."

Emma shut her eyes against the planted image. If the awful things she'd seen today didn't keep her up all night, the thought of Sawyer in the shower absolutely would.

They loaded more of Emma's and Henry's things into the SUV and hit the road at twilight. By nightfall, they were settled in at his place, and Henry was fast asleep. Emma carried the baby monitor back to the living area after putting Henry down for the night.

"That was fast," Sawyer said, looking impressed.

"He was exhausted," she said. "I hope he doesn't remember any of this when he gets older."

Sawyer's lips turned up in a small, sad smile. "He won't. Most people don't have memories until pre-school, and those are fuzzy."

Emma sighed. He was right. Her earliest memories were around age five. So, maybe Henry would have a chance at normal, and the things he'd experienced this week might not turn him into a neurotic, anxiety-riddled mess. "Do you think whoever trashed my house will be back?" she asked.

Sawyer seemed to consider the question for a long beat. "He overturned everything in sight. I'm not sure there's anywhere left to look at your place. Hopefully, he's satisfied that whatever he wants isn't there, and he'll leave the house alone."

She wrapped her arms around her middle and rubbed the goose bumps off her skin.

"Are you hungry?" Sawyer asked, moving toward the kitchen.

Her stomach growled audibly in response. The only person who'd eaten anything since breakfast was Henry, who'd never missed a bottle.

Sawyer washed up at the sink, and Emma found herself staring.

"Why don't you let me cook this time?" she asked. "I saw some trout in the refrigerator this morning. There's plenty of veggies for a salad. You can shower while I get dinner started. We can meet on the deck for dinner."

Sawyer lifted his brows and straightened his shoulders. "I accept."

SAWYER RUSHED THROUGH a lukewarm shower, hurrying to clean up and get back out there to guard and enjoy Emma before she fell asleep.

Fifteen minutes later he pulled a plain black T-shirt and his most comfortable blue jeans over still-damp skin, and ran his fingers through wet hair. He peeked in on Henry before heading down the hall in Emma's direction. He found her on the rear deck, lighting candles along the railing. The table was set with a tossed salad in the center and ice water at each place.

"Trout will be done soon," she said, looking him over from head to toe with an expression that bordered on hunger. When her eyes met his, she blushed.

Sawyer's blood heated. She was checking him out. "Everything looks great," he said, "and dinner smells delicious." The familiar pinch of conflict warred in him. He wanted desperately to tell her how he felt and work out every detail of what would happen to them next.

Unfortunately, Sara was still missing, and they weren't any closer to finding her, naming the killer or figuring out what she'd been up to. So far, Sawyer had failed his mission. If there was a worse time to attempt to woo a woman, he couldn't think of one.

Emma opened the grill and tested the trout with a fork, then squeezed a lemon over the tops of the fillets, and levered each off the grates and onto a serving dish.

They ate in silence. Fireflies hovering over the lake. Moonlight reflecting on the silver water. The tension between them seemed to grow exponentially, and Sawyer realized it might be bad news in the making. Emma pushed the food around her plate, rarely making eye contact. Was she getting up the nerve to let him down easy? Had she seen the way he looked at her and known it was best to nip this in the bud? Was she trying, in her own sweet way, not to hurt him when she gave him his walking papers?

Sawyer set his fork aside, no longer hungry. If he was right, it would explain her attitude earlier, when he'd suggested buying a second crib for Henry to use at his house. *Maybe she didn't plan to let Sawyer see him long enough at a time to necessitate a crib.*

That couldn't be right.

Could it?

Emma wiped her mouth and set the napkin aside. "Can we talk?"

"Yes." Sawyer frowned, prepared to vehemently plead his case. No, he hadn't returned her message when he'd gotten home, and he understood now that he should have, but he was trying to do the right thing by letting her go. He thought she'd moved on, and he had no right to barge back in, in search of something that was no longer there. Of course, he didn't know about Henry then, but now that he did, he'd never walk away from his son.

Sawyer didn't want to walk away from Emma either.

She flopped back in her chair, the hem of her shirt knotted around her fingers. "We need to talk about the crib situation and my behavior earlier."

Sawyer dragged his chair around the table and captured her fidgeting hands in his, overcome with the need to stop her from saying the words that would break him. "Me first," he said, swallowing his pride. He couldn't let her push him back out of her life until she knew how he felt. If she still wanted out after he'd spilled his guts, he couldn't stop her, but at least she would have all the facts before making a huge decision. "I should have called," he said.

Her mouth opened, then slowly shut without a protest.

"I was trying to do the right thing, but I can see now how wrong it was." He lifted her hands in his and pressed them to his lips. "Emma, you are the only reason I'm even here today. Thoughts of you were what got me through my darkest times. The memories we made together kept me fighting when I wanted to give up." He squeezed her hands. "I needed to get back here to you like I'd promised I would. Now here I am. I'm home. A civilian and a father."

Emma blinked. "And? What are you saying, Sawyer?"

"I'm saying that I don't know what kind of arrangement you have in mind for us with Henry in the future, but I'll accept whatever terms you give as long as I can be with him as often as possible. I've already missed too much. I don't want to miss another thing. Not his first word or first step. Not his first baseball game or fishing derby or car or college…"

Emma sniffled. "Sawyer."

"Wait." He steeled himself for the finish. He was only halfway there, and he needed to finish before some other calamity kept him from it. "Once I'd made it back on base, away from the insurgents who'd held me all those months, I thought things would get better, but they didn't. Being physically safe seemed to shift the stress. Once I was no longer in survival mode, I had time to think. And it's all I did, but then I had a hard time concentrating on anything other than what I'd been through. I couldn't eat or sleep. I retreated into my head with the memories I didn't want. It was like falling into a black hole every day. By the time I made it back stateside and was discharged, I was spinning out of control. My team at Fortress helped. They kept my head on straight. Gave me renewed purpose. New missions to save lives. My guys checked on me, made sure I toed the line and wasn't slipping back into the darkness, and it made all the difference. I was only beginning to feel human again when I took your call the other night, but I hadn't felt like myself in a year before that. It was like I'd been lost at sea and you were the lighthouse. I saw your face, and everything changed."

Emma blinked fat tears over her cheeks. She lifted her hands to her mouth and released a small sigh.

Shame racked Sawyer. He never wanted to be the reason for her tears, and he certainly hadn't meant to burden her with his troubles, only to open up to her so that she could understand. "I want you to be happy, you and Henry, even if that's not with me. Just…be happy."

Her expression hardened, and she folded her arms. "Why wouldn't I be happy with you?"

He frowned. "Didn't you hear me? I'm a mess.

A barely recovered nightmare who just promised to protect you a few days ago and has failed repeatedly."

"That's not true," she said, setting her jaw and shifting her weight.

His gaze slid to the angry purple-and-brown bruise across her cheekbone.

"I was mugged outside a credit union," she said, apparently knowing where his thoughts had gone. "No one could have predicted that. *No one.*"

He opened his mouth to tell her that was his job. To troubleshoot, to think ahead of the danger and keep her away from it, not stand across the street while she was assaulted and pretend it could have happened to anyone. He'd been lax, and it had cost her.

She raised a palm to stop the interruption. "You've done nothing but protect me every minute since you got here, so don't try to tell yourself or me otherwise, because I'm not buying it."

Sawyer's mouth snapped shut. He watched the hard line of her narrow jaw clench, and despite himself, a pinch of misplaced pride swept through him. He loved that fire in her. The spark for justice when she thought something wasn't fair or right. The internal defender. Emma was kindness and honor, love and determination. She was all the things he aspired to be, and seeing her so ready to defend him sent a wave of warmth and hope through his chest.

"You haven't failed me," she said. "Not once. Not even when you got home and decided not to return my message. I can be hurt that you didn't call, but it won't change the fact that I would've done the same thing in your position. I would've tried to protect you from me too, and I would've done exactly what you did."

Sawyer's heart clenched. "What?"

"I think you are a brave and honorable man, Sawyer Lance. I don't want you to ever think any differently. I'm proud to know you, and I'm proud that you are my son's father. I was only upset about the crib earlier because I didn't like the idea of dividing Henry between us. It sounded like you wanted to split custody, but I don't want that."

Sawyer raised his palms to cup her beautiful face. A reed of hope rearing in him. "What do you want?"

She fixed emotion-filled eyes on his. "You."

Sawyer closed his mouth over hers, unable to contain himself any longer.

He kissed her slowly, deliberately, until she was breathless and unsteady in his arms, then he carried her inside.

Chapter Thirteen

The next two days went quietly. Too quietly. No news. No new leads. The few times Detective Rosen called with updates, the information had changed nothing. Security footage of the hit-and-run outside the credit union confirmed the vehicle was a rental registered to Mr. Harrison, but there was no clear shot of the driver. Kate had regained consciousness and was doing much better, but she hadn't gotten a look at the driver either. Sawyer suspected it hadn't been Harrison behind the wheel, but considering the bank manager had been murdered, there was no way to know for sure now.

Detective Rosen had also let them know a hospital in the next town had reported a male gunshot victim. The man's wound was consistent with one delivered by the gun Sawyer had used on the intruder sneaking through Sara's window. Unfortunately, the shot had been a through and through, and there was no way to definitively connect that man's injury to Sawyer's gun. Since Sawyer never saw his face, and couldn't identify him anyway, the man was released after providing a bogus story. The local detective was supposed to follow up with him. His blood was being sent to a lab where it would eventually be tested against the blood collected from Sara's windowsill.

None of this got them one step closer to finding Sara, and time was marching on. Six days had passed since she'd been dragged from her home, and Sawyer still had no idea who could have done it, or where she could be. Worse, Emma had been right that first night when she'd said the odds of finding her sister would diminish significantly after the first seventy-two hours.

He reached for Emma in the dark bedroom. He'd fallen asleep with her in his arms again, feeling happier and lighter than he had in a year. He could get used to what they had going, and he was determined to ask her to stay with him once he'd returned her sister safely. Sawyer knew that rescuing Sara wouldn't bring his fallen teammates back, but it would be a great step in regaining his peace.

Emma rolled against him, her long hair splayed over his pillow and her warm breasts pressed to his chest. He longed to take her again, but that was no surprise. He never stopped wanting her. He'd always thought the month he'd had with her when they met was perfect, but he'd been wrong. Hearing Emma tell him that she wanted him and that she was proud he was her son's father, *that* was perfect.

Sawyer stroked her hair and kissed her forehead

before settling back onto his pillow, smiling and thoroughly content.

Moonlight streamed across the ceiling, and he was immeasurably thankful for the rest he'd gotten these last two nights with Emma. Though he wasn't sure what had woken him this time. Another nightmare? He didn't think so. He couldn't recall dreaming. Henry? Sawyer set his senses on alert and listened hard in the darkness. His son's breaths came deep and steady through the monitor. Henry was fast asleep, but instinct tugged at Sawyer's chest the way it had when someone had been in Emma's house with them that night.

Sawyer rose onto his elbows and forearms, a sense of dread erasing the peace he'd had only moments before. A heartbeat later he heard it. The low growling of a small engine. Maybe even an ATV like the intruder at Emma's house had escaped on.

Sawyer slid out of bed and dressed quickly in the darkness, listening closely to every creak, breath and heartbeat within his walls. The growl drew closer, and he cursed as an unfortunate realization struck. He hadn't heard an ATV. He'd heard at least three.

"Emma," he whispered, nudging her shoulder. "Wake up."

She jolted upright, eyes glazed with fatigue. "Henry?"

"No," Sawyer said. This was much worse. "We've got company."

Emma scrambled out of bed and pulled one of his

T-shirts over her head, making an instant dress that stopped midthigh. "What's happening?"

Sawyer slid steady fingers between the panels of his bedroom curtain and peered into the night. Emma slid in front of him. Four single headlights cut through the dense and distant forest. All were headed toward Sawyer's home. "Call the police." Sawyer gripped Emma's shoulders and turned her to face him. "Get Henry and hide," he said. He snagged his sidearm from the nightstand and tucked it into his waistband, then pulled another from a drawer and kept it in his right hand.

Emma dialed and pressed the phone to her ear. "I don't know where to hide," she said, moving toward Henry's crib. "I don't know what to do."

Sawyer dropped the curtain back into place. She had a good question. He'd never had to hide before, certainly not on his own property, and he had no idea what to tell her.

"Hello," she said into the receiver, "this is Emma Hart, and I need help." She rattled off an overview of the last few days with mention of the four ATVs headed their way.

Sawyer handed her the keys to the rented SUV. "Get to the truck and drive to the police station."

"What about you?" she asked, gathering her sleeping baby and his blankets into her arms, the cell phone clenched between her shoulder and cheek.

"I can handle four men, but not while keeping an

eye on the two of you. You need to stay safe. Protect Henry. I'll focus on the intruders."

"I'm so sick of running," she said, frowning fiercely.

The debate was cut short when the ATVs went silent outside.

Sawyer parted the curtains again. The headlights were out, and the world was silent. They'd abandoned their vehicles. "They're moving forward on foot," he said, turning back to Emma once more.

She slid into her shoes and disconnected the phone call. "Local police are on the way," she said. "Dispatch is calling Detective Rosen for us. They'll fill him in on what's happening now."

"Good work." Sawyer ushered Emma down the hall toward his back door and pressed his back to the wall. Emma followed his example. Together, they watched a foursome of armed silhouettes drift across the lawn in the moonlight, heading for the front porch. Sawyer gave Emma a reassuring look. "I'll take care of them. You and Henry head for the SUV," Sawyer whispered. "Get in and drive. Don't stop until you reach the local police precinct."

Emma gripped his arm, unfathomable fear in her big blue eyes.

He set his hand over hers. "It's going to be okay. Get yourself and Henry to safety." Sawyer squeezed her fingers, then slid into the night, hating himself for leaving her behind, but it was for the best. Sawyer was well trained, but there was only one of him, and he had no idea who these men were. They could be former military or even mercenaries for all he knew. To be safe, Henry and Emma needed to get as far away as possible. The intruders had come via ATVs, which they'd left a significant distance away from the house. Even when they heard the SUV spark to life, there would be little they could do to stop it.

Sawyer jumped over the handrail at the side of the porch, steering clear of the motion sensing light, then crept around the side of his home, gun drawn.

Frogs and crickets sang in the grasses and near the lake. A sky full of stars arched overhead. The same stars he'd watched through the corner of a filthy window during the nights of his captivity. He pushed the memory aside and listened for the gentle stir of the SUV engine.

He stilled to listen as whispered voices rose to his ears. "You get the girl and the baby," one man said. "I'll take out the bodyguard."

Sawyer's jaw locked. *No one* was getting his girl or his baby. He lowered into a crouch and cut through the shadows like a lion after its prey, determined to stop them, incapacitate them, hold them until the police arrived, whatever the cost.

A brilliant, silvery moon came and went behind a mass of fast-moving clouds overhead. Memories of his last night-strike forced their way into his head. His pace slowed as the earth shifted beneath him. The scene morphed and changed before his eyes. Suddenly he was in uniform, outside an enemy stronghold in dangerous territory with his team behind him. He felt the drip of sweat slip from beneath his helmet and ride over his temple to his jaw. Saw the guards up ahead. Militants. Two at the door. One on the roof. One on patrol. He hadn't known about that one before. Sawyer stumbled to a stop. He blinked and rubbed his eyes, willing the images to clear, willing his heart rate to settle, his concentration to return. He sipped cool night air and cursed himself inwardly. He thought he'd put these episodes behind him. Thought his mind was on the mend.

One of the four trespassers came into view, keeping watch along the home's edge. The others had gone ahead. This was their lookout, and Sawyer had the element of surprise on his side. He could drop the man with a single shot. Not a kill shot, but one that would put him down and keep him there. The sound would pull the others from the home, and if it went well, Sawyer could lie in wait, hidden in the shadows, plucking them off one by one until he had a pile of bleeding criminals awaiting the arrival of local law enforcement. If it went poorly and they split up before coming outside, Sawyer could find himself surrounded.

He sighted his handgun, choosing the least lethal, most effective shot. But the memories returned, and his weapon grew unsteady in his outstretched hands. His finger grazed the trigger, then pulled back. Touched, then relented. During his last mission, it had been the sound of his fire that had given away their approach. He had gotten them captured. Gotten his team killed.

Sawyer's tongue seemed to swell, his throat tightened. He lowered the gun and shook his head hard, as if he might be able to clear his thoughts physically. He had to move. Had to do something. The others were surely inside by now, and Sawyer still hadn't heard the SUV's engine ignite. He had to act. He couldn't afford not to. His breaths were quick and shallow as he crept through the night, closing in on the nearest target.

The distinct sound of the back door caused his heart to sprint. The normally soft metallic click was like an explosion in the night.

The man before him turned. His curious eyes went wide at the sight of Sawyer a mere foot away.

Sawyer's gun was up on instinct, stopping the man from raising his, but Sawyer couldn't force his finger back to the trigger. He couldn't feel his fingers or toes. Fear had wrapped him like a wet, heavy blanket, and the knowledge he wasn't in complete control was enough to make him want to run.

But soldiers don't run.

He braced himself. Forced down the fear. Even as the dark world shimmied and brightened around him.

A sinister grin curled the man's lips, and he lunged.

"Dammit," Sawyer whispered, opening his stance and accepting the weight of the wild, untrained attack.

Three quick moves later, the thud of the man's falling body brought Sawyer back to the moment, and images of that long-ago night were shoved away. *One down and three to go.*

EMMA HELD HENRY close and listened to the night. She had the SUV keys in one palm and her shoulder pressed against the back door of Sawyer's home, preparing to run. All she had to do was find the courage.

The SUV was parked in the gravel drive twenty feet away. It would be simple, under normal conditions, to cross the small porch, hop down the short flight of stairs and be at the vehicle in seconds, even carrying Henry.

But these weren't normal conditions, and Emma's heart was seizing with panic at the thought of making a run for it now. She'd seen the silhouettes of the trespassers as they'd approached, and they were armed. She couldn't dodge or outrun a bullet, and she couldn't bring herself to risk Henry's life by trying. Her mind urged her to hide, not run. Hiding had saved Henry on the night of Sara's abduction and again on the night the intruder had broken into Sara's room. Hiding worked for them.

Running was a dangerous unknown.

Behind her, the front door opened with a heavy creak. Soft footfalls spread through the house, forcing her onto the back porch.

Help is on the way, she reminded herself. *The local police are coming.*

She released the screen door behind her, eyes focused on her goal. The SUV. She dared a small step forward, but something held her back. The tail of Sawyer's oversize shirt was caught in the door. Emma bit her lip and willed herself to remain calm. The moment she let panic take over, she'd make messy, potentially deadly decisions.

Henry squirmed in her arms, his small features bunching.

"Shh, shh, shh," she cooed.

The footfalls inside drew closer, headed her way.

Emma jerked forward, freeing herself from the door with a quiet thwap! She flew down the back porch stairs on silent feet. The motion light flashed on as she reached the base of the steps. The short distance to the SUV warped and stretched before her like a dream where the hallway never ended and no matter how hard or fast she ran for the door, she wouldn't arrive.

Move, she begged herself. *Run.*

The back door opened, and Emma scurried into the shadows against the house. It was too late to make a run for the SUV in the bath of security lighting. She'd missed her moment. Running now would only put a massive target on her back *and Henry's*.

She crouched alongside the porch, careful to keep her head low, and she scanned her dark surroundings.

"Where are they?" a man growled.

"I don't know," another man answered. "The car's here. They couldn't have gone far."

Emma listened to the footfalls as they paced the

porch. She ducked deeper out of sight as the men approached the railing at her side.

"Check the house again," the first man said. "Where are your brothers?"

There was a long pause. "I don't know," the second lower voice said.

"Well, find them!"

One set of footsteps headed back into the house and out of earshot. The other man lingered. Waiting. Maybe even sensing she was near.

Emma watched as he leaned over the railing's edge and scanned the darkness. He was dressed in head-to-toe black riding gear, like the man who'd cut the brake lines on Sawyer's truck and chased them through the national forest. This man didn't have a helmet, but she still didn't recognize his face.

A chilly autumn breeze whipped through the air, and Henry made a small discontented sound.

Emma jumped back, jamming her bare legs into the thorns and briars of bushes along Sawyer's home. She bit her tongue against the stings of instant bruises and cuts and pressed a steadying kiss to Henry's once again crumpled expression.

Her baby's eyes fluttered shut and pinched tight as he tried to hold on to sleep.

The porch boards creaked.

The man was coming.

Emma broke into a sprint through the night, clutching Henry to her chest to absorb the impact of her flight. He squirmed but didn't cry.

She paused at the front of the house. Where could she go? Not onto the deck, dock or lake. She peered at the dark forest across the field. The men had come from the forest on the opposite side of the home. Was this tree line safe? Or was it possible more bad men lurked there, as well? How many were there? *Where were they?* she wondered, nearly frozen with fear once more.

"Did you find them?" an angry voice asked. The sound echoed in the night, near the opposite end of the house now, but any one of the four men could be on her in a second.

"No," another low male voice answered. "No sign of the lady, the baby or the guy. I didn't find my brothers either."

"Come on," the other voice said. "We'll split up and circle the place. You go that way. I'll go this way. We'll meet in the middle."

Emma sucked in a hard breath. She had to move. If she ran for the trees, they'd spot her crossing the field. The SUV was far away now, on the opposite end of the house. Behind her, near the voices.

A new fear breached her thoughts. Where was Sawyer? Where were the man's brothers? Did Sawyer have them, or did they have Sawyer?

She pushed the thoughts aside. One problem at a time. Right now, she was on her own to save Henry, and that started by staying hidden and alive until the local police could arrive. She scanned her options once more, looked into Henry's precious face, and made her decision.

"I love you," she whispered against Henry's soft hair. "You stay still, and I'll do everything I can to protect you."

As if in acceptance of their deal, Henry gave a soft snore.

Emma counted down from three, then she hurried across the short lawn toward the water. She slowed at the sandy bank, choosing her footing carefully so there wouldn't be footprints to follow. She took easy steps into the cold water. Fall's shorter days and colder nights had taken hold of the lake, despite unseasonably warm days. She sucked air as she waded deeper, to her thighs, her bottom. Then she carried Henry toward the dock and pulled a large red-and-white cooler from the weathered boards. She took it with her beneath the dock.

Carefully, she placed Henry and his mass of blankets into the cooler, onto the sand- and dirt-lined bottom.

Satisfied the makeshift boat would hold up, she ducked beneath the dock, sinking to her shoulders in the frigid water, and floated Henry along with her.

Ripples moved across the previously serene surface, a hundred neon signs pointing out their escape route.

Emma held as still as possible and anchored the cooler in place before her. She closed her eyes, hoping the ripples would stop before the men came to examine the lake.

A frog jumped nearby, making a little splash. Henry squirmed in the cooler.

"Shh, shh, shh," she soothed, holding the little vessel as it rocked on the ripples ebbing around her.

His tiny lips formed an angry frown, though his eyes were determinedly closed.

"Did you hear that?" a man asked. The harsh whisper startled Emma with its nearness. "I think I heard something near the water."

Emma gripped the cooler, hating herself for choosing the worst hiding place in the world. If they spotted her, she couldn't even run. She hadn't saved Henry and herself. She'd made them easy targets.

Two sets of feet pounded onto the deck above them.

Emma cringed. Her heart raced, and her stomach lurched. She lifted a desperate prayer as her fingertips nudged the soft rubber tip of Henry's pacifier caught in the blanket folds. She plugged it into his twisted mouth and stiffened every muscle in her body, willing her baby to be silent and the ripples to stop announcing her presence.

"No boat," one of the men said, taking a few steps closer.

The second man paced overhead. "I'm sure I heard something."

"Fish," his partner muttered, "ducks, bats, frogs. Who cares? We've got to keep looking."

The weight of their combined retreat rattled the boards, shaking dirt onto Emma's head. She stretched a palm over Henry's slowly wrinkling expression.

"Achoo!" Henry sneezed in a tiny puff of air.

The men froze. "What the hell was that?"

"What?"

Emma could see their faces through the space between boards now. She could read their murderous expressions and see their hands on their guns. All they had to do was look down, and her life was over. *Henry's* was over. His little boat couldn't save him from a bullet.

Her limbs and lips began to tremble. Her teeth rattled hard in her head. Tears welled in her eyes.

Bang! Bang! Bang!

A trio of gunshots erupted in the distance.

And Emma's heart thunked hard and heavy.

She'd already lost her parents and possibly Sara. Had she just lost Sawyer, as well?

Chapter Fourteen

The men on the dock lurched into desperate sprints, arms and knees pumping, guns drawn as they raced toward the sound of gunfire.

Henry flailed in his little boat, then broke into tears. The violent cries were masked by a shoot-out. Emma inched through the water, away from the dock, away from the muzzle flashes and gunshots on the west side of Sawyer's home, the same side where the intruders had left their ATVs. A rush of unexpected pleasure drove through her as she realized a gunfight meant Sawyer was still alive and conscious out there somewhere.

The jolt of happiness propelled her to action. She moved more quickly through the water, towing Henry carefully back to shore.

His temper quieted slightly as she pulled him into her arms and left the cooler in the water to sink. His little breaths came hard and fast, and his bottom lip trembled, puffing in and out with each raspy gasp, but for the moment, the wails had stopped.

Emma ran in sopping, squeaking sneakers toward the woods on the opposite side of Sawyer's house, away from the national forest, the intruders and the gunshots. Hot tears stung her icy cheeks as she flew through the night, stumbling on frozen legs, her wet skin screaming from the chill of blowing wind. Could Sawyer hold off four armed men on his own? For how long? How much ammo did he have on him? How much had he already expelled?

Where were the local cops?

Her hand went to the phone tucked into her bra, intending to call 911 and check on the cavalry, but the icy feel of her shirt slid through her heart. Her phone was gone. Likely lost forever at the bottom of Lake Anna.

The night was suddenly still. Quiet. No more shots fired. No sounds of a struggle.

Nothing.

Emma sent up a prayer and kept moving.

Soon, the low and distant cries of emergency vehicles and first responders pricked her ears. A moment later a much nearer sound wound to life. The familiar growl of ATV engines fading quickly into the night.

She stopped. Turned back. What did the sounds mean? Had the shooting stopped because the intruders heard the sirens and fled?

Or had the shooting stopped because they'd killed Sawyer and would come for her again the moment the police left her unattended?

Her heart ached with the possibility he could be

gone. "Sawyer," she whispered. Surely it couldn't be true. She stepped back toward the house, drawn by the need to know he was okay.

She didn't want to know a world, or a life, without him in it. It wasn't fair. It wasn't right.

A hot tear fell from her eye to Henry's forehead. Startled, his arms jerked wide. His lips curved down in the perfect angry frown.

"Sorry, baby," she whispered through a growing lump in her throat.

"Emma!"

Her name boomed through the night.

She lifted her gaze to the house, senses heightened. "Sawyer?" she asked the darkness.

"Emma!" he hollered again, this time closer, his voice intent and demanding. "Emma! Come out. It's clear." The silhouette of a man appeared beneath the cone of the security light as he passed the back porch.

"Sawyer!" Emma gasped. "Here! We're here." She started back across the field at a jog. *He was okay.*

Sawyer ran at her, arms wide. "Emma," he croaked. "I thought I'd lost you." He stroked her hair and kissed her face.

She bawled ugly tears of joy.

Henry screamed. He'd had enough of this night. He was outside after bedtime. He'd been floated in the water. Put inside a cooler. Had his little eardrums tested by a gunfight.

"The gunfight," she said, teeth beginning to chatter. "What h-happened?"

Sawyer pulled back with a questioning frown. "You thought I'd lose a gunfight?"

"There were four of them," she said. "I h-heard dozens of sh-shots."

"I only shot four times," Sawyer said. "I missed twice. It's tougher than you'd think to hit a man dressed in black who's running through the night." He wrapped his arms around her and rubbed her frozen skin for friction. "I hit one in the leg before he got to his vehicle, and I hit the other's ATV before he drove away. The rest of the shots you heard were all theirs missing me. I took down the first two men hand to hand. They're out cold where I dropped them. The other pair fled."

Emergency lights cut through the night as a line of first responders rolled along the gravel drive to Sawyer's home.

Henry, Sawyer and Emma were safe again for now.

Sawyer pulled Henry into his arms and held him tight, then looked carefully at Emma for the first time. "Did you fall in the water?" He glanced back at Henry, who was completely dry.

"N-n-no." She considered where to start the story, then told it as quickly as possible while trying not to bite her tongue or break her teeth from all the shivers and chattering.

SAWYER FELT HIS blood boil as he listened to Emma retell the events that had forced her into frigid waters with their infant son. He pulled her a little tighter, wishing that he'd been there for her instead of across the property, letting two trespassers get away.

The side yard teemed with activity when they rounded the corner. Two cruisers and two ambulances were parked behind an unmarked SUV, presumably the detective on duty. Sawyer led Emma toward the ambulance.

"Oh, sweetie." An older heavyset woman rushed to meet them outside the open ambulance bay doors. Her sweet spirit and nurturing nature were evident in her kind eyes and audible in her gentle tone. Sawyer relaxed by a fraction. The woman reached for Emma, ushering her to the ambulance. "You look like you're freezing. Come here. Let's get you warm." She caught a blanket by its corners and stretched it in Emma's direction, opened wide to wrap around her patient's trembling shoulders. "That's a start," she said, motioning Emma toward the vehicle. "Hop in so I can fix you up," she said.

Emma's teeth chattered. "H-H-Henry,"

The woman's expression faltered. Her warm brown eyes snapped in Sawyer's direction, hyperfocused on the blanket in his arms. "Was the baby hurt?"

"No," Sawyer said with confidence. If he had been, it would've been the first thing she said.

Emma shook her head. "He's just t-tired and sc-scared."

Sawyer rubbed the blanket covering her back. "Let her look you over. I've got Henry," he promised. "We're fine."

The older woman tipped her head and refreshed her smile. "I've got heated blankets and dry scrubs in the bus."

Emma nodded woodenly, pressing her lips into a thin white line.

Sawyer kissed her head, then helped her into the ambulance.

"We'll only be a moment," the woman said before pulling the bay doors shut.

Sawyer leaned in, listening through the panels.

"Here you are. Go ahead and change out of that wet shirt, then I'll get your vitals."

Sawyer breathed easier. Emma was in good hands. Now he'd find out who the four trespassers had been. He'd knocked two of them out cold. Maybe at least one of them would talk. He frowned at the spot on the lawn where he'd left the first man unconscious. Hopefully, he'd been collected by the local officers and put in cuffs somewhere for safekeeping.

"Mr. Lance?" A man in jeans, a T-shirt and ball cap called from his porch.

Sawyer changed directions.

The man was Sawyer's age give or take a few years. His boots were unlaced and there were creases on his cheeks, signs he hadn't been on duty when he'd gotten the call to come tonight. The sleep marks were also indicative of a deep sleep recently interrupted. Sawyer couldn't help envying a man who was able to sleep so deeply that the sheets had left marks that were still visible. Sawyer had only truly slept soundly a few times in the better part of a year, each of those times had been this week, always with Emma in his arms.

Sawyer shook the man's hand. "Sawyer Lance."

"Detective Steven Miller," the man said. "I spoke with Detective Rosen on my drive over, and he brought me up to speed. Were you or Miss Hart harmed tonight?"

"No."

His gaze slid to the blue bundle in Sawyer's arms. "Was your son?"

"No," Sawyer said, feeling his protective hold on Henry tighten. Was this the way Emma felt all those times he'd noticed her pulling Henry a little closer? "Emma's with the EMT right now."

The detective's mouth turned down. "How many trespassers were here tonight?"

"Four," Sawyer said, turning his attention toward the spot in the yard where the first man he'd knocked out had landed. "I left one right over there, and another in the hallway outside my bathroom. Two got away on the ATVs they rode in on." He raised a hand in the direction where the vehicles had been. "I hit one vehicle and one driver. A superficial leg wound. I'd aimed for the tires, but the trees are thick, and they were moving fast."

"And it's the middle of the night," Detective Miller said. "How far away were you?"

"About thirty yards."

The detective gave an appreciative whistle. "I'd say you did all right."

"What happened to the man I left outside?" Sawyer asked, avoiding the detective's next logical question. *Where did Sawyer train to shoot like that?* It wasn't a deviation in topic he wanted to take right now. Right now, he wanted facts and answers.

"Outside?" Miller shook his head. "We only found one man. Inside."

Sawyer opened his mouth to swear, then shut it. His gaze dropping to the infant in his arms. He'd never been one to take issue with cursing, but it just felt wrong to be the one introducing his baby to the words. "I guess he got away." Though he wasn't sure when. Sawyer hadn't seen a third headlight when the other two men fled, and he hadn't heard another engine rev to life after the other had run off. "I don't suppose you recognize the man you found in here?" he asked.

"I do," Miller said.

Sawyer felt his brow raise. "Is that right?"

Emma jogged in their direction and up the steps to Sawyer's side, dressed in pale blue scrubs that dragged the ground and sagged off her shoulders. She wound her arms around his middle and pressed a cold cheek to his chest. "I'm fine," she said, rolling her eyes up to his. "Shaken up and cold, but well. How's Henry?"

"Perfect," Sawyer answered. "This is Detective Steven Miller. Detective Rosen filled him in on the case."

The detective extended a hand in her direction and they shook.

Emma gave him a slow and careful look, stopping to examine the badge on Miller's belt. "I didn't mean to interrupt. You said you recognized one of the men?"

A uniformed officer appeared, tugging a man in cuffs along at his side.

"Yep." The detective raised a palm, halting the cop and criminal. "Miss Hart, Mr. Lance, this is David Finn, an occasional visitor at the local police department. Petty crimes mostly."

Sawyer ground his teeth, aching to knock David Finn back into unconsciousness for about a week.

"Your last name is Finn?" Emma asked, releasing Sawyer and squinting up at the scowling man and his big black eye.

"Yeah? So?" he snapped.

Emma chewed her bottom lip. "I just wanted to hear him talk," she said. "This isn't the man who mugged me or took my sister. His voice is all wrong, and it's not the man who broke into Sara's room. Sawyer shot that guy."

David Finn slid his gaze to Sawyer, and Sawyer smiled.

He reached for Emma, bringing her back against his side.

Detective Miller gave Finn an appraising look. "So, what's your big important role in this mess, Finn? How do you fit into the business of terrifying this nice family? You're certainly not the muscle," he said with a wicked grin, circling a finger in the direction of the man's swollen eye. "And I'm still trying to figure out when you graduated from graffitiing the corner store to the attempted murder of a new mother and her infant."

"Man," Finn drawled, "I didn't attempt murder on nobody. I didn't even touch that woman or her baby, and I ain't talking to you until I talk to a lawyer."

Miller motioned the uniform to take Finn away.

As they passed, Emma pressed closer to Sawyer, a small tremor playing in her hand on his back. "I heard his voice when I was hiding," she said. "He was looking for his brother or brothers. David had family here tonight. Why?"

David craned his neck for a look back as the officer hauled him down the steps. He didn't speak, but the fear was plain in his eyes. David knew Emma knew about his brothers, and they weren't getting away like he'd thought. That truth gave Sawyer a measure of satisfaction.

It also worried him to know that by failing the mission, the sloppy foursome had turned their target into a witness.

Emma rubbed her palms against her arms, still fighting the cold.

"Why don't we go inside?" Sawyer said. "You're probably chilled to the bone, and Henry will be more comfortable in his crib, away from the wind."

Emma nodded. She looked to Miller. "Can you stay for coffee or tea, Detective?"

He took a long look at the scene beyond the porch. The ambulances and cruisers were packing up and pulling out, leaving his unmarked SUV alone beside Sawyer's rental. "Why not?" he said. "I'll be hanging around until the crime scene crew gets here to collect empty casings from the shoot-out. I might as well warm up while I wait."

"Great," Emma said, her spirits seeming to lift a bit.

Sawyer held the door for Emma and Miller, then followed them inside. "Is there anything I can do to help tonight?" he asked. "Finding the casings, identifying the tread marks or tracking the escape route?"

"Nothing tonight," Miller said. "I'd like to have you both speak with a sketch artist tomorrow if you're willing. Anything you can remember about the fourth man's face. I have photos of the Finn boys you can use to identify which ones were here tonight."

Emma nodded. "Okay." She led the way into the kitchen and stared at the counter. "Tea or coffee?" she asked.

"Coffee," Miller said. "Black."

Sawyer stopped to admire the limited number of scratches on the front door's dead bolt. "One of those men knew how to use a lock pick."

"Yep," Miller responded. "Probably the one you saw leaving in handcuffs. Petty theft is his idea of a good time."

Sawyer stared at the lock, hating what an easy mark he'd made Emma and Henry. He'd assumed the fact that his home was registered to the company, in another county and had only recently become a place with an address would be enough to keep them safe for a few days. He ran a freaking private protection company, and he'd failed to lock down his own home.

Sawyer excused himself to put Henry in his crib, then headed back to the kitchen. When the sun rose, his place was getting a security overhaul that would be worthy of his company name.

Emma lined mugs on the counter where his old coffee machine puffed and grunted against the backsplash. "Will Detective Rosen be out tonight?" she asked Miller.

"No." The detective scanned Sawyer's home casually as he spoke. "Rosen said he's got his hands full back in Knox County. Seems the sudden crime spree over there has taxed their force to the limits, and he's barely treading water."

"How much did he tell you about my situation?" she asked.

Miller tipped his head over each shoulder briefly. "He says your sister found and documented evidence of an embezzlement scheme at her credit union. Someone was pulling hundreds of thousands of dollars a year out of the accounts by manipulating the computer system."

Emma shot Sawyer a pointed look. "That's a lot of money."

"Did he say how they were doing it?" she asked, filling three mugs with coffee and ferrying them to the table in a tight triangle between her palms.

"Computers," he said. "Someone manipulated the program that determines the interest owed on folks' accounts. The system began directing a small portion of the interest earned into an offshore account. The interest owed on most accounts is only about one-and-a-half percent, and the portion diverted from each account was minuscule at best. Most people didn't notice a few extra dollars or cents gone. Most probably didn't bother to do the math on it, just trusted the bank to add their one-and-a-half percent every quarter. In the event someone noticed and called the credit union on it, a correction was made immediately, and those accounts were credited fifty dollars as restitution for the error. Then that account was removed from the list of accounts being attacked."

"Then Sara noticed what was happening," Emma guessed.

Miller took another long pull on the steamy black coffee. "According to Rosen, she started looking at every account. One by one."

Sawyer smiled, watching Emma's face light up at the mention of her sister. "That's Sara," she said, "and it explains the mass amount of numbers in her notebook."

Detective Miller sat back in his seat. "Your sister tracked every error and the date the error was made for the past twelve months, logged the details, built a case to show the credit union's interest program had a flaw. Then, somehow, she managed to get her hands on the matching offshore account numbers, and Rosen thinks that was when things changed. Probably, whoever she looked to for help was high enough up the food chain to have been part of the scheme she'd uncovered. She sounds like a smart, determined, resourceful woman."

"She is," Emma said. "I wish Detective Rosen would have told us all this. He knows I want to be kept in the loop, but he rarely calls. It's infuriating."

Miller finished his coffee and set the mug aside. "It's a lot of information, but none of it brings you any closer to your sister, and I think Rosen's hoping to call with news that matters. Men like Rosen and me got into this for the people. I'm guessing he doesn't give two flips about bank interest. He's working to get Sara home." He offered a small smile. "I wish I was officially on that case because it sounds a world more interesting than the junk I deal with over here in Tennessee's most rural county."

Sawyer rubbed a palm against the stubble covering his cheek. He lived in Tennessee's most rural county, on a finger of a lake sandwiched between two forests. "How do you think these guys found us out here tonight?" It had taken emergency responders at least ten minutes to arrive, and they knew exactly where to go. The remoteness, Sawyer realized, was great until he needed the authorities, then he'd have to be prepared to wait.

Miller cast a look at Emma, then back to Sawyer. "Rosen's men have been searching Miss Hart's land, looking for the bullet that went through the man you shot earlier this week. If they find it and match it to their suspect, they can arrest him. They haven't found the bullet yet, but they did find a listening device late this afternoon. You'll be hearing from him tomorrow about a sweep of the home's interior for additional devices."

Sawyer moaned. "The man with the duffel bag came to plant bugs while he snooped."

"Seems like."

Emma paled. "We talked about Sawyer's home while we cleaned. The lake. Our time here."

Detective Miller frowned and pushed to his feet. "I'd better get out there. See if I can find some of the casings from tonight's showdown. Match the bullets to the guns. Guns to their owners."

Sawyer followed Miller to the door. "Before you go, what can you tell us about David Finn and his brothers?"

"Not a lot. The Finns are a big family, and they keep to themselves. Dad's a mechanic. Mom stays home with all the kids. They're strapped for cash most of the time like a lot of folks around here. Some of the older boys have been in trouble from time to time, vandalism, shoplifting, petty theft. Nothing like this."

Sawyer mulled that over. "When you say the Finns are strapped for cash, how strapped are you talking?

They don't have enough money to take the whole gang out for ice cream after T-ball, or they don't even have enough money for the kids to play T-ball?"

"More like the church delivers gifts every year so the kids have something to open on Christmas morning."

A whoosh of air left Emma's chest as she appeared at Sawyer's side. There was sudden and profound sadness in her eyes. "So, David and his brothers were likely the hired henchmen," she said. "Coerced into participation by their need to assist the family."

Detective Miller cocked his head. "It's nice of you to jump to that conclusion. I'm not sure most would in your position."

Sawyer smiled. Emma's kind heart and compassion were two of his favorite things about her.

Emma looked at Sawyer. "What?" Her brows knit together. "Most people are good," she said with finality. "What wouldn't you do to feed your family?"

Sawyer considered ticking off a list. *Murder. Theft. Kidnapping.* But he wasn't sure. Wouldn't he steal to feed his son? Wouldn't he kill to protect his wife? Mother? Brother? The honest answer was that it would depend on the circumstances. That he honestly didn't know. He'd never, thankfully, been in the dire straits Miller described. He'd never been in the Finns' shoes, so he couldn't judge, but he'd like to think that he'd always side with the law.

Detective Miller's cheek kicked up in a lazy half

smile as he watched the exchange between Emma and Sawyer.

Emma's shoulders drooped. "I'm not trying to make excuses for criminals," she said. "At the risk of sounding awful, David Finn didn't look, sound or carry himself like someone with a lot of education, motivation or discipline. So, I doubt he's the criminal mastermind behind all this. Couple that with his family's financial situation, and it's more likely that he's made a bad decision for what he sees as a good reason."

Miller slid his gaze to Sawyer and smiled. "She's observant."

Sawyer laughed. "Yes, she is. I also noticed that the leather riding gear they wore was high-end, and those ATVs were new."

"So, either this wasn't the Finn brothers' first job," Emma said, "or the one in charge bought new bikes for his crew."

Sawyer gave her hand a squeeze. "That's my guess."

"New bikes?" Miller asked. "Did you get a make and model?"

"Yeah." Sawyer grabbed a pen and paper, then jotted down a description of the vehicles. He stopped suddenly, a smile spreading over his face. "Emma and I saw four headlights in the trees when the men arrived. Four bikes. Four men."

Emma smiled. "David didn't leave on his ATV."

It was still out there.

Miller swung the door open. "Nice work." He

tipped two fingers to the brim of his ball cap. "I think I'll go see about that vehicle. I should be able to find the owner through the registration or purchase order. Thank you for the coffee."

"Detective Miller," Emma said, rushing to catch him before he slipped back into the night. "Wait."

Miller stopped on the threshold and raised his brows.

"Did Detective Rosen say if there has been a new lead on my sister?"

The detective took his time answering, but Sawyer saw the slight sag in his shoulders, the downward curve of his mouth. No news. "No, ma'am, I'm sorry," he said finally.

Emma blew out a soft breath. "Okay, well…" She looked at the floor, at her hands, scrambling for something more. "Is there any chance that the Finns have her? Could they be keeping her somewhere?" she asked. "Maybe hiding Sara has been their role in this until now. If they were being paid to keep her hidden, the payoff might've been enough money to buy the ATVs and riding gear."

Sawyer slid an arm around her back, eyes locked on Miller. Was it possible? "Is there someplace on the Finns' land where that could be possible? There were three brothers here tonight. That's more than enough muscle to contain one injured woman."

Detective Miller paused. He scooped the ball cap off his head and ran his fingers through messy hair. "It's a big property," he said. "Family land. I haven't been there personally, but I hear it's land-locked. Good for hunting and not much else."

"No neighbors, then," Emma said. "Secluded."

Miller rubbed his chin. "I suppose much of it is. I'd need a warrant to go poking through the home or property."

Emma stiffened against Sawyer's side. "Does that mean you think I could be right? Do you have enough evidence to get a warrant?"

He tugged the cap back on, swiveled it just right. "Not yet, but I'll call the station, see if the officers were able to get David to talk, and I'll take a look at the ATV left in the forest. If I can get a confession or link the Finns to the embezzlement scheme or something else connected to your sister, I'll have enough to wake up a judge." He smiled and stood a little taller. "I'll see what I can do."

Emma grabbed onto his hand as he turned to leave. "Thank you," she breathed.

Sawyer folded Emma into his arms and kissed her head. What she'd asked of the detective was a long shot, but it was something.

Chapter Fifteen

Sawyer curled Emma against his chest. She'd showered until her skin was hot and pink, then dressed in sweatpants and a sweatshirt and crawled into bed fighting a tremor. He'd kissed her head and shoulders and wrapped her in his arms until her rigid muscles relaxed. When he'd felt her soft, easy breaths on his arm, he knew she'd finally found sleep.

She jumped around 3:00 a.m. when the sound of crunching gravel announced that Miller and the crime scene crew had finished searching the forest for clues and were on their way out. One officer stayed behind, keeping watch indefinitely at Miller's request.

"It's okay," Sawyer whispered. He stroked her cheek with the back of his fingers, careful to avoid the yellowing bruise from her mugging, and he snuggled her a little tighter. "I've got you."

Emma shimmied in his arms, rolling to face him with sleepy blue eyes. "Do you think Detective Miller will be able to get the warrant?"

"I hope so," Sawyer said.

He kissed her forehead and gave her a warm smile, but he hated that the first idea they'd had about where Sara might be was just a guess. It was the first hope they'd had, and after all the bad things that had already happened, he worried about how Emma would handle it if this theory didn't pan out.

Emma didn't speak again for a long while. She drew patterns on his chest with her fingertips, leaving heated trails over the fabric of his shirt. "The judge might not think there's enough cause to issue a warrant."

Honestly, Sawyer didn't either. Not yet. "I know." Sara could be with the man who took her and not with the Finns, or she could be at a site not directly related to any of the people they knew were involved. She could be anywhere.

Emma rolled back an inch and looked up at him in the darkness. "What if you and I take Henry to see the Finns in the morning?"

Alarm struck through Sawyer at the thought of Emma going within a mile of that family. "I don't think that's a great idea."

"Why not?" she asked. "If Detective Miller can't get enough together to justify a warrant, maybe we can. We can stop by and introduce ourselves to the parents, let them know we're the family their sons broke in on last night, and that my sister's missing. We can tell them we're worried about her, and we're only there to see if they have any idea who their sons have been spending time with lately. Not to accuse them of anything. Maybe they'll talk to us. They might be defensive toward policemen, but mother to mother, Mrs. Finn should understand my fear and want to help me if she can."

Sawyer rose onto his elbow and rested his cheek in his hand. "I wouldn't want to do anything that could tip the other boys off," he said. "They know David was caught tonight, but they might not know that we know they were here with him, or that we're considering the possibility that Sara is being kept on their land. Knocking on their door and introducing ourselves could set off all the alarms, and if she is there, our appearance could be enough to make them move her. Personally, I don't like a plan with that much risk," he said. "Not with Sara's safety on the line. Not to mention, we don't want to muck up whatever Miller and Rosen are doing."

Emma dropped her head in frustration. She rolled back over and settled against him before falling asleep once more.

Despite her nearness and the steady sounds of Henry's breaths in the crib beside his bed, Sawyer didn't sleep. He wouldn't sleep until his home was secure and all the men involved in the break-in were behind bars. Instead, he spent the hours until dawn devising a way to keep Emma safe while getting a look at the Finns' land without upsetting the case authorities were building.

THE NEXT DAY was long and quiet. Sawyer arranged an early-morning delivery of enough security equipment to thoroughly lock down the cozy A-frame home. He upgraded the ruined security system and added a feature that would cause flashing lights and an earsplitting alarm in the event of tampering. The chaos would confuse an intruder long enough for Sawyer to drop him. He'd learned the hard way that a system that only alerted the police wouldn't be enough. His home was simply too far from the nearest police station.

After lunch he changed the locks and dead bolts on the doors, and reinforced the jambs to protect against an intruder intent on kicking his way in. Emma stopped him from putting bars on the windows, so he ordered bulletproof glass to be delivered in three to five business days. In the meantime, he set up cameras and a silent alarm system along the property's perimeter that reported to his main computer inside.

Emma spent the day playing, cuddling and napping with Henry. She'd eaten all her meals with Sawyer, but hadn't had much to say, except when Detective Miller had arrived with a sketch artist, eliminating their need to make a run to the station. Miller walked the property while Sawyer and Emma did their best to describe the men they'd seen last night. Afterward, Miller had brought her a surprise. Her cell phone was in the bushes along the house, dropped in her escape from the trespassers, instead of in the lake, where she thought it had gone.

Once Miller and the artist left, there was only endless silence. Whoever said no news was good news had clearly never had to wait on something.

When Emma slipped into the shower after dinner, Sawyer moved onto the back porch to call the detectives. He started with Detective Miller.

Sawyer gave the trees around his property another long exam. He doubted he'd ever forget the mess they'd been through last night, and he knew Emma wouldn't. Maybe it was time to return the A-frame to the company and look for a place to put down roots with her and Henry. A place where they could make happy memories. Someplace near parks and good schools. Maybe Emma would help him find the perfect spot to raise their son together, if he didn't screw everything up.

"Miller," the detective answered.

Sawyer made a quick pass through the formalities before getting down to business. "Anything new since you left this afternoon? Were you able to get David Finn to talk, or have you traced the ATV to its owner?" Ice fingers dug into the hair at the base of his neck, then slid down his spine. Sawyer rolled his shoulders and stretched his neck, throwing a cautious eye toward the trees.

"Nah," Miller said. "Finn's not talking, but I located the store that sold the ATV."

"Great," Sawyer said, standing straighter.

"You'd think." Miller grunted. "The purchase order says the buyer paid cash for the bike left in the trees last night. The camera over the register is a dummy, and the teenage sales clerk doesn't remember what the customer looked like because that was the night her boyfriend broke up with her and she vowed to never notice another man again. She only answered the few questions she did because I had a badge."

Sawyer dragged a hand over the back of his neck and gritted his teeth.

"The sales receipt recorded the date and time of the pickup, so I've requested security footage from nearby businesses around that time. We might get lucky and catch a glimpse of the truck hauling the ATV away. If I can get a plate on the truck, I can follow the registration back to the owner."

Sawyer crossed his arms and scanned the distance again. "Any chance you got that warrant?"

"Based on what I've got?" he asked. "No. I don't have anything to link Mr. and Mrs. Finn to Sara's abduction. David might be their son, but he doesn't live with them."

"Where does he live?"

"Ratty apartment downtown. No signs of Sara," Miller said. "I checked last night."

Sawyer said his goodbyes, then dialed Rosen.

Rosen was equally unhelpful, but he confirmed the listening device Miller said had been found on Emma's property. He thanked Sawyer for the message Emma had left earlier providing verbal permission to sweep the house for additional bugs, along with directions to find the hidden key kept in their greenhouse. He had a team out there now.

Sawyer wandered back down the hall to his room, a little defeated, and waited for Emma to finish in the shower.

"Goodness!" Emma gasped upon sight of him on the floor with Henry. "What are you doing?" She pressed a palm to her chest as she lowered herself beside them.

"We're playing airplane," Sawyer said, passing their son her way with some enthusiastic jet sounds. "You look beautiful," he said, dropping a kiss on her nose. "How are you feeling?"

She shrugged. "Hopeful, I think. I'm almost glad those guys came for us here because now we have the power of two county law enforcement groups helping us look for Sara."

Sawyer scooted closer. "I had an idea. Now that I've got this place locked down, except for the window bars." He narrowed his eyes at her.

She bumped her arm against his. "That was a ridiculous suggestion."

"It wasn't a suggestion. The bars are in the closet now."

Emma smiled, her head shaking. "Go on with your new idea, please."

"I think the men who were here last night are probably regrouping and planning their next move. One was definitely shot, and I don't know how big this crew is, but that makes two with a GSW inside three nights, so now might be a good time for us to make a move."

Emma settled Henry on her lap and fixed a curious look on Sawyer. "What do you have in mind?"

Sawyer filled her in on the calls he'd made while she showered, then he suggested what he'd been weighing all day. "I want to gear up and head over to the Finn property at dusk, alone."

Emma squinted. "What does that mean?"

"I don't want to knock on their door. I don't want to give them the chance to say no. I want to enter the Finn property at its most remote access point, walk the land, look for outbuildings, abandoned mine shafts, anywhere big enough to hold Sara. I want you to wait here with Henry. You'll be safe if you stay inside, and Miller's got a lawman stationed on the property in case you need him."

Emma cuddled Henry close. "You're going on a rescue mission."

"Yes." The idea of Sara being held against her will had weighed on him more heavily every day. He knew that pain and understood those complicated feelings too well. The heartbreaking belief that no one was coming. The guilt and remorse. Sawyer's decision to shoot the night guard had alerted other unseen enemies, ultimately leading to the capture, torture and murder of his teammates. Sara, no doubt, blamed herself for pursuing the issue at her credit union. "If

I find her, I can bring her home. The police can't even look."

Emma set her hand against his cheek and pressed her forehead to his. She sucked in an audible breath.

"I won't go if you don't feel one hundred percent safe here without me. You and Henry are my top priority."

Emma sniffled softly, then pressed her lips to his, drawing a deep, involuntary groan from him before she pulled away. "Go," she said with a smile. "Find Sara. We'll be right here waiting when you get back."

Sawyer got to work immediately, dressing in black and gathering his weapons and ammo. A sidearm in his belt holster. A spare at his ankle. A duffel bag with night-vision goggles, smoke bombs, wire cutters and anything else he thought might help him on his mission. "I might be a while," he said. "Could be past dawn. I pulled the topography map off the county auditor's website, and there's a lot of ground to cover."

She gripped his wrists in her small hands, a fervent look on her beautiful face. "Just come back to me," she said. "I love you, Sawyer Lance, and I don't want to spend another day without you in my life or in Henry's. We're your teammates now."

Sawyer's heart swelled. "I will come home to you," he vowed, "and if Sara's anywhere on those hundred or so acres of Finn land, I'm going to find her, and I'm bringing her home." He slid his arms around her and delivered a deep and assuring kiss before stepping onto the porch. "I'll wait while you set the alarm."

Emma nodded. She punched in the code, and the little activation light flashed red. *Armed.*

Sawyer let the officer patrolling his property know he'd be gone awhile, then he jogged to the rented SUV and climbed behind the wheel. Twilight was upon him, but he had a map and a twofold plan: search and recover. Return home to his new team.

NIGHT FELL SLOWLY over Emma's temporary home. She put Henry to bed around ten and knew he'd stay there dreaming contentedly until dawn. She, on the other hand, doubted she'd be able to sleep until she saw Sawyer's face again. There were so many things she should have told him. Her heart was full and warm with the knowledge that while she'd retreated into her head for the day, and he'd locked the house down like Fort Knox, he'd also been plotting a way to help her sister.

By two thirty in the morning, her nerves had gotten the best of her, and she set a kettle on the stove for tea. The pot whistled, and Emma went to pour herself a little chamomile tea. She tried hard to keep her mind off the possibility that Sara would come home tonight, but hope was stubborn, and she'd thought of little else since Sawyer had gone to look for her.

She filled a cup and inhaled the sweetly scented steam as she raised it to her lips.

Poised to sip, the lights flickered.

Emma braced herself against the counter and waited, listening to the wind whistle around the windows.

A moment later the lights flickered again.

Moving to the door, phone in hand, she dared a look outside for the officer on guard duty. When she didn't see him in his car, she dialed the number he'd given her when he'd arrived for his shift.

The officer didn't answer.

Her heart rate kicked into double time.

Sawyer had secured the home today. He'd barred the door. Installed a high-tech alarm system that would contact the police if the power lines were cut or anyone broke in while the alarm was set, which it was. He'd made every provision short of window bars or bulletproof glass, she reminded herself She was safe as long as she didn't go outside.

She stared hard into the night, willing the patrolling officer to appear. Maybe he'd dropped his phone without realizing or had left it in his cruiser while making a sweep of the perimeter.

The tall grassy field beyond the glass waved to her in the moonlight. Trees arched and stretched. Fallen leaves spun in tiny tornadoes around the yard, but there were no signs of intruders. No growling ATVs. No telltale headlights or silhouettes of armed men. *Just the wind.*

She dialed the officer again. Maybe he'd just missed the call.

The lights blinked out before the call connected,

leaving her in the dark as the call went to voice mail once more.

"We're safe," she whispered. "This is fine. Only a brewing storm." She turned from the window, determined to stay calm. Sawyer had worked on the home's wiring all day, replacing the security system, installing new lights and sirens. The wind had probably just knocked something loose.

But she couldn't explain away the missing cop.

She brought up 911 on her phone and debated.

A loud pop turned her toward the hallway. The sound was loud and strange. Like nothing she'd heard before and very close. The newly installed security lights began to flash in the hallway and living area. An alarm blared in short, sharp blasts. Gnarled fingers of fear curled around her heart and squeezed.

Henry!

Emma ran down the hallway to the bedroom, slightly disoriented by the intense, repetitive bursts of light and sound. Her phone's flashlight beam streaked the walls and floor ahead of her as she gripped the room's doorjamb and propelled herself inside.

Light from her phone fell over an empty crib.

"No." Air rushed from Emma's lungs in a painful whoosh. Her mouth dried. The muscles of her stomach gripped. *This couldn't be happening. It wasn't possible.*

"Henry!" She swung the beam around the room. There were no security lights in the bedrooms, and the continuous flash from the hallway only added to her fear and unease.

The picture window beside the bed was shattered, cracked into a thousand individual crystals, most of which were now on the floor, glittering under the beam of her light. *This was the sound she heard.* Someone had broken the glass, and taken Henry.

"Henry!" she screamed, flashing the phone's light wildly through the space. She ran to the window in search of someone taking off with her son outside.

Instead, she found the missing officer. Facedown and unmoving in the grass.

"Henry!" Her scream became a sob. Sawyer had taken the only vehicle. She was trapped. Alone. Helpless.

Emma turned the phone over in her palm and hit Send on the call she'd had at the ready.

"Nine-one-one, what's your emergency?" A tinny voice echoed across the line.

"Someone kidnapped my son," she said, working to calm her labored breaths. She couldn't report the crime if she had a panic attack, went into shock or passed out.

"What is your name?" the dispatcher asked. "And where are you now? I'll send someone immediately."

Henry's cries broke through the intermittent blares, and Emma spun back toward the hallway. "I don't think I'm alone," she whispered.

"Are you saying there's an intruder in your home?" the voice asked. "Ma'am? Where are you?"

A sudden scream sent Emma into the dark hallway, sprinting frantically toward the sound of her son.

"Ma'am?" the voice asked. "I need your name and location."

"My name is Emma Hart," she rasped. "I'm at a cabin on Lake Anna off of Pinehurst by the national forest." She slid to a wild stop on socked feet at the end of the brightly flashing hall.

Before her, a large man blocked the way. Tall and lean, he towered over her, making the baby in his arms seem impossibly more fragile.

"Henry," she whispered.

"Hang up," the man said. "Now."

Emma disconnected the call.

The man stepped closer. He wore the black leather riding gear she'd come to know and loathe. He also wore a ski mask. "Put the phone down." The eerie calm in his voice was familiar and impossibly scarier than any sound she'd ever heard. This was the man who'd taken Sara.

Henry kicked and arched his back in a fit of fear and anger.

Emma dropped the phone where she stood, outstretching her arms. "Please. Give him to me." Her voice quaked. Her eyes burned and blurred with tears. She couldn't allow this monster to have her son. "I'll do whatever you want. Just don't hurt him."

The man motioned her toward the door. "I'd hoped you'd say that." The sinister curl of his lips was visible through the ski mask. He liked her fear, she realized. This was an elaborate game to him.

And he would kill her when he finished playing. Her. Sara. And Henry.

"Now, turn off your alarm."

Emma pried her dry, pasty mouth open and willed her words to be level and calm. "The alarm is wired to all points of entry. Windows included. When you broke it, you caused an alarm. Someone is probably already on their way."

He pulled a handgun from behind him and pointed it at the number pad, easily balancing her baby in one hand and the firearm in the other. "Shut it off."

Emma's windpipe narrowed. She obeyed, praying the emergency call she'd made, coupled with the broken window, would bring help fast. She pressed the numbers on the keypad carefully until the red light flashed green. "It's off," she said, turning back to the man, arms outstretched once more. "Please," she begged.

"Outside." He pointed to the door.

Her stomach coiled, and her mind raced. She needed to get her hands on Henry. Needed to make a run for the woods or the road, get away and hide until help could arrive.

"Out," he repeated, this time with venom.

Henry screamed again, a loud, maddening demand nearly as loud as the siren she'd recently silenced. It was pure fear. Pure agony, and Emma felt each new cry in her soul.

"Okay." She choked. "Okay." She slid her feet into sneakers by the door and pulled back the security bar, flipped a line of new dead bolts, then moved into the windy night.

On the living room floor behind them, her cell phone began to ring.

"Go." Her abductor pressed the hard barrel of his gun against her spine and forced her ahead.

"To the trees," he growled. "And don't try anything stupid, or I could get confused and drop this squirming kid. I might even step on him while I'm trying to get my hands on you."

Emma lifted her palms. "I won't," she whimpered. "Just, please, don't hurt him."

"Move."

"Where are we going?" she asked. "Are you taking us into the forest to kill us?"

He sniffed a laugh. "I could've killed you in your house," he said.

"Why didn't you?" She moved as slowly as possible with the gun against her back. The pressure of it bruising her spine. If she wasted enough time, maybe help would arrive.

Emma watched the horizon for a sweep of blue and white lights against the darkness, desperate to hear the racing sirens.

The weeds grew taller with every step away from Sawyer's neatly manicured lawn. Sticks and weeds brushed against her legs and clung to her shoes. Bristles and briars tore at her skin.

Beyond the first rows of trees, a black ATV waited with a rifle attached to a gun rack on the back. "Get on," he said.

"I don't know how to drive," she cried, confused and desperate. "There's nowhere for Henry."

The man moved in close. "Get on the bike, and you'll get your baby."

Emma scrambled onto the seat, arms reaching, tears falling.

As promised, he placed her son into her arms. She pulled Henry against her. His small body was cold from the blasting wind. He was dressed in one-piece terry cloth pajamas, no coat, no hat. The psychopath who took him hadn't even taken his blanket from the crib to warm him. Emma hugged and shushed and kissed Henry before turning back to the man with the gun. "I can't hold him and drive. He can't ride on this. It's not safe."

The man fastened the strap of a helmet under his chin, then gripped Henry's thin arm in one black gloved hand. "Fine, we'll leave him here."

"No!" Emma screeched, panic racking her chest at the thought of leaving her infant on the forest floor. What was wrong with this man? Who could be so cold and damaged?

"Move forward," he demanded, shoving her with his free hand.

"What?" Emma rearranged Henry in her arms, nuzzling his cold face against her warm neck and trying, uselessly, to shield him from the gusting wind. She looked at the narrowing seat and gas tank between her and the handlebars. "Where?"

The man swung one long leg over the padded area behind her, and she instinctively scooted up.

Her thighs gripped the icy metal of the tank.

The man leaned against her back, reaching around her for the handlebars and doubling her over in the process, his chest against her back, Henry clutched precariously to her torso. The engine revved to life, and the man kicked the beast into gear.

Henry gave a pained scream as the vehicle jolted into the night, his protests swallowed by the roaring engine beneath them.

The ATV slid around curves, throwing earth into the air as it bounded over hills and flew along paths nearly invisible to Emma. She clutched Henry to her, willing him to be safe, whatever happened next.

She couldn't imagine where they were being taken, or what the man's plan was for them once they got there, but Emma knew it wasn't good. Her tears fell hard and fast, blown from her eyes by the raging, frigid wind as they tore through the darkness, one slender beam of light to guide the way.

Chapter Sixteen

Emma lost track of time, clinging to the bike for her life and to her son for his. Her face, arms and legs were numb from the biting wind, and Henry shook wildly in her arms. She kept her eyes and mouth closed as much as possible, fighting against the fear and nausea, trying to keep herself together for when they stopped. Whenever that might be. She peeked, occasionally, in search of something she could use to orient herself. A landmark for location or a ranger's office for help when she was able to get free.

The only thing she saw were trees.

Eventually, the ATV slowed. The engine quieted to a purr, and the force of raging wind became something more endurable. Henry's screams were audible once more.

The driver climbed off the machine, chilling her back instantly where his body heat had warmed her. She struggled to straighten, thankful for the coldness that meant he was away from her, and she could arrange Henry more comfortably in her arms. The moon was bigger, brighter where they were now. On a mountain devoid of objects to block or filter the light.

Before them, the headlight illuminated a large ramshackle shed. There was nothing else in sight except trees and the collapsed remains of a home long ago given back to the forest. A thick metal chain and padlock hung strong and new around the shed's aged door handles, and another powerful round of fear pricked Emma's skin. Someone was storing something of great value.

Sara.

"Get up," the driver barked as he approached the barn. "This is the end of the road for you."

Emma swallowed hard. She climbed awkwardly off the bike and stood on numb, trembling legs.

Her captor turned to the building. His attention shifted to the lock.

This was Emma's chance to run. She twisted at the waist in search of an escape path. The forest was dense around her, and the slopes were steep in every direction, covered in rocks, leaves, twigs, a thousand things to trip on, fall over in the night. The path behind them was relatively clear, but her abductor had an ATV to give chase. Even without the bike, he was undoubtedly stronger, likely faster, and unlike her, he'd dressed for the weather. Even if she managed to stay out of his reach, she couldn't hide. Not while carrying a screaming baby.

"Let's go," the man snapped as the lock gave way. "Inside."

Emma swallowed hard. She couldn't move. The dilapidated shed suddenly looked more like a tomb. The fine hairs on her arms and neck rose to attention. She was certain that going inside meant never coming out, and she refused to sign her son's death warrant.

He wrenched the heavy lock off the loosened chain and thrust the door wide. "Inside," he repeated. "Now."

Emma shook her head, arms tight on Henry, lips trembling. She'd made things bad enough by getting on that bike. She couldn't keep obliging this criminal. The bully. The killer.

He turned on her. "I said…"

Emma ran.

Her feet pounded the earth, flying wildly over the path the ATV had taken, away from the shed and the man who'd forced her out of Sawyer's home at gunpoint. Heart pounding, mind reeling, she searched the darkness for a way off the path and into the trees without falling over the sharp cliff on one side or trying to climb the hill on the other.

Bang! A shot rang out, echoing through the hills and evacuating a thousand bats from nearby trees. Henry screamed.

Emma slowed, raising one palm like a criminal in surrender while holding Henry tightly with the other.

A heavy hand clamped over her shoulder and spun

her around, shoving her back in the direction of the shed. The armed man stayed behind her. His thick angry fingers dug into the back of her neck and the flesh of her shoulder. He swore vehemently as he steered her to the open door.

She dug her heels into the earth as her baby cried and flailed in her arms. Terrified of what she'd find inside.

The man gave her another shove, and Emma stumbled forward.

She recognized the shadowy form on the filthy wooden floor immediately. "Sara."

Sara shifted, raising her face to squint at Emma. Her arms and legs were bound, her face bloodied. Clothes ruined. What had he done to her? "Emma! No!" Sara cried. "No." She slung a line of thoroughly emasculating swears at her captor, then spit at his feet.

He dealt Emma another powerful shove, and she lurched forward, across the threshold and onto her knees.

She released Henry with one hand to brace them against the fall, and her wrist gave a gut-wrenching crack upon impact. Shards of blinding light shot through her vision as the pain spread like a heat wave over her body.

Beside her, moonlight shone through a hole in the roof, lending an eerie glow to the horrific scene before her. Sara sobbed and begged their captor for

Emma and Henry's safety. She was a thin and fractured mess. Bruised and battered, filthy and frail.

The man unzipped his jacket and reached inside.

Emma scrambled back, angling Henry away from the man and placing herself in front of Sara. "No!" she screamed, imagining the gun already pulled. "Don't!"

He produced a cell phone with one hand, then unfastened the chin strap on his helmet with the other. He removed the helmet and ski mask as he walked back through the door.

Emma held her breath, watching intently as he tucked the helmet under one arm and pressed the cell phone between his ear and shoulder. She shushed Henry and cradled her probably broken wrist, avoiding eye contact as the man turned back to close the door. His face flashed into view a heartbeat before the barrier slammed shut, and Emma's blood ran cold.

Christopher. The man who'd stood in for Mr. Harrison at the credit union on the morning the police had found Mr. Harrison's body. Christopher had probably murdered him, then rolled in for a day of work like nothing was out of the ordinary. He'd been cool, calm and collected when they'd spoken at nine thirty that morning. Her stomach lurched at the memory of his easy smile. It went beyond unhinged to something more like completely deranged.

Sara sobbed against the rough wooden floorboards, apparently half-out of her mind with fear and pain. Her face was battered and caked with dried blood. Her wrists and ankles were raw from the ropes used to bind them.

Emma crawled to her sister's side and gently laid Henry on the floor with her. "It's going to be okay," she whispered, low enough to keep the hope between sisters. "I'm here. We're together now, and we're going to be okay." Emma wasn't sure she believed the words, but they had always been true before. She was counting on them to be true now.

Sara shook her head, frantic. "He'll kill you. You aren't bound yet. You have to run."

Emma hooked her fingers into the ropes at Sara's wrists and tugged with her good hand. Her left hand. Her weak and uncoordinated hand. Nothing happened.

"Stop," Sara said, tears spilling over too-pale cheeks. "You've got to find a way out of here."

Emma relented. Sara was right. Christopher could return at any minute. "Okay."

Outside, the ATV engine kicked to life and slowly moved away.

Emma checked the door. Locked. She examined the hole in the roof. Too high. Nothing to climb on.

"I'm so sorry," Sara gasped. "It's my fault you're here. It's my fault you're hurt. That Henry's hurt. I tried to protect you from all this."

Emma gave Henry a long look. "I don't think Henry's hurt. He's just scared. Cold. Mad." She backed up to get a better look at her sister and their jail cell, then levered Henry into her arms to comfort him. Her wrist screamed from the motion.

"I should have told you what I'd been up to," Sara said. "Then you could have told the police everything right away."

Emma shook her head and gently shushed her baby. "I would have done the same thing."

"I found discrepancies at the credit union," Sara said. "I thought the system was miscalculating interest, but it wasn't an accident. Christopher was stealing."

"I know," Emma said, circling the small room. She needed to find a way out of the shed before Christopher returned. No windows. One chained door. One hole in the ceiling out of reach.

"The accounts weren't just being shorted a portion of their interest. The missing interest was actually being diverted to an offshore account."

"I know," Emma repeated. "I gave your notebook to the police. We figured out what was happening, but no one knew who was behind it or where to look for you." She cuddled Henry closer, and his cries begin to soften. "Now I know it was Christopher."

Sara nodded. "Christopher works in IT at corporate. He wrote the program that stole the money. Harrison helped me figure out what was happening when I brought my notebook to him. We downloaded all the evidence we needed to contact the police, and I saved it on a thumb drive hidden in the picture frame on my desk at work, behind the photo of us with Mom and Dad." She blinked back another round of tears. "I wanted to keep you out of this to protect you, but all I did was put you and Henry in danger."

Emma pressed an ear to the wall and listened. Silence. "I have that photo," she told Sara with a grin. "It's on the mantel at Sawyer's house. The evidence is safe." And best of all, the lunatic who mugged her for the diaper bag of Sara's things hadn't gotten it.

Sara stilled. Her eyes went wide. "Sawyer Lance?" She slid her gaze to Henry. "*The* Sawyer Lance?"

"Yeah." She pressed her good hand to the door and moved clockwise around the room in search of a weak link. In a cabin older than time, complete with chunks of missing roof, there had to be a board somewhere weaker than her. "I'll catch you up as soon as we get out of here." She pressed the toe of her shoe against the base of every wall board where it met the floor, testing the integrity of each dark spot for signs of rot. "Come on," she whispered.

Sara wriggled upright on the floor, calming like Henry and beginning to regain herself. Her tears were gone, and a fresh fire burned in her eyes. "You have the evidence," she said. "That means we can put Christopher in jail for a long time for embezzlement after we get out of here. Harrison will testify."

Emma sighed. "Harrison was murdered."

"Murdered?" Sara's lips parted in horror. "How?"

"Gunshot. Someone tried to make it look like a suicide, but they failed. I assume it was Christopher, but he has a crew of goons working with him now."

"The Finns," Sara whispered. "They bring me food and water."

"Yeah. I think there are others too. In the week that you've been gone, Christopher has added a lot to the embezzlement, including multiple counts of breaking and entering, a hit-and-run, tampering with brake lines, three counts of abduction, a mugging and assault." She thought it over. "The brake line thing might qualify as attempted murder, same with the hit-and-run."

Sara gasped, "What has been happening out there?"

"Nothing good," Emma said, reconsidering immediately. She'd been reunited with Sawyer. Henry with his father. She was in love. Those were all good things. And the thought of Sawyer sparked a new idea in her head. "Do you know if we're on Finn land?"

Sara nodded. "I think so."

Emma smiled. "Sawyer left at twilight to come here and search for you. He hasn't found you yet, which means he's still on his way." And that was very good news. "He must've covered a lot of ground by now. It's only a matter of time before he finds this shed."

She gave the next board a kick, and her foot broke through. "Here!" Emma kicked again. Then again. The wood crumbled and splintered under the force. Slowly the initial shoe-size hole expanded into something big enough to slide Henry through. Soon, they would be able to run.

"Keep going," Sara said, scooting in Emma's direction. "When it's big enough for you to get out, go. Get help."

Emma turned her attention on Sara as she continued to kick and press the decrepit board. "I don't want to leave you."

"I can't go," Sara said. "I can't run. My feet are bound."

"Maybe we can find a way to cut your ropes."

"No," Sara snapped. "I can't go, but you can. We always put Henry first. That's the rule, and we never break it. So, you'll take him and go. Come back with help."

Outside, the low rumble of an ATV returned, growing louder with each passing second.

Emma's gaze darted around the room in search of something sharp to work on Sara's binds, but she was right. There was only dirt and wood. Her next kick wrenched the board loose with a crack, and Emma lowered quickly to the floor. She planted both feet against the edges of crumbled wood and pushed. The planks snapped and groaned under pressure. Hunks of the wall fell into the grass outside, and Emma's feet were suddenly beyond the cabin. Her hips and shoulders would fit through, as well.

"You did it!" Sara said. "You did it! Go! Take Henry and run!"

Emma pulled her feet back and hurried to Sara's

side. She threw her arm around her sister's back and hugged her tight, not knowing if it would be the last time she'd ever see her. The painful tightening of her chest, lungs and heart was nearly enough to make her stay. "I love you," she whispered. "You are my best friend. My sister. My hero. Always have been. Always will be."

The ATV arrived, and the engine was silenced.

Sara batted tears. "You be the hero tonight, okay?"

Emma nodded. "Okay." She kissed her sister, then turned for the newly made escape hatch.

Before she could cross the small space to safety, the chains rattled and the shed door swung open.

Chapter Seventeen

Christopher ignited a flashlight, briefly illuminating his angry face. His helmet and ski mask were off, his hair messy from the aftereffects of both. He swung the beam of light over the floor in search of his captives. Shock tore through his scowl as the beam stopped on the generous hole Emma had recently kicked in the wall.

"What the hell?" he snarled, storming inside the dank and musty shed, fists balled. "Did you do that? How the hell did you do that?"

Emma stiffened, scooted back, but didn't speak. A tremor rocked over her limbs and coiled her nerves into a spring. She'd been hit by him once, outside the credit union, and she'd seen him strangle Sara. She knew what he was capable of, and she hated herself for not being faster on the escape. She'd been so close. Another minute, and she and Henry would've been hidden in the shadows, on their way to find help.

Christopher squatted for a closer look at the

hole, then turned to Emma with his signature sinister smile.

She swallowed hard, scrambling for an explanation, contemplating a run for the door. Though running from him hadn't gone her way the last time.

He jerked to his feet, and Emma angled away, blocking her battered sister from his view. "Let us go, and we won't tell anyone what you've done," she begged. The plea was little more than a whisper on her sticky, swollen tongue, her mouth dry and pasty with fear.

Christopher barked an ugly, humorless laugh. He pulled his phone from one pocket and stared at the illuminated screen. "In case you haven't noticed, I don't make deals," he said. "I give orders and I call the shots."

She imagined his inflated ego swelling until it lifted right through the hole in the ceiling. "Then what do you want from us?" she asked. "What's the point? Why did you bring us here?"

He stepped purposefully in Emma's direction, and she winced.

He smiled wider.

Emma widened her stance and prepared to dodge him if he reached for her, or duck if he swung. She breathed easier when he stopped moving and checked his phone. Still, she had no idea why he'd taken the three of them and delivered them to the godforsaken shed. If not to kill them, which he could have already done, then why?

Christopher returned the phone to his pocket, looking satisfied with whatever message he'd received. He leaned at the waist, cold blue eyes searching for Sara around Emma's side. "I worked on this for years, then you just jumped right in and ruined it. You couldn't let it go. You had to pursue it. Relentlessly. Even after you called corporate to report the problem, and I told you I'd handle it. You just couldn't let it go!" His tone grew louder and more hostile with every word.

Emma glanced at her sister's equally red face.

Sara glared past Emma to Christopher. "You're tech support. I called you for help with what I thought was a system glitch. I had no idea I'd contacted the person who'd created the problem," she said, "at least, not until the problem never cleared up."

"You weren't supposed to follow up! That's not your job!"

"You're just tech support?" Emma asked, recalling Christopher at the credit union in a suit and a smile.

"I'm not *just* anything. Except smart, rich and fed up," he snapped. "Harrison wouldn't confess to his part in the ongoing amateur investigation with your sister, even under threat of death, and you saw how that went for him. I used my corporate ID badge to pass as the stand-in manager because I needed access to Harrison's office computer to remove any evidence he kept there. I got that job done, but there's still the issue with Sara. She told me she has enough data to ruin me, but she won't tell me where it is or who she's told. Funny, because she had a real big mouth when it came to shouting the problem from the rooftops."

"I was trying to help people," Sara cried.

Henry gave a grunt and squeal of complaint against the angry voices.

Christopher blew out a breath of exasperation. "This could have all ended with you. I asked you who you told, and you lied. Now all these deaths are on your head."

Who did you tell?

The vicious whisper from Emma's memories rocked her back on her heels. She swallowed another lump of hate and remorse. "I was there," she said. "When you came into our home and tore her away. I heard you hit her. Choke her. Saw you slam her onto our couch and climb on top of her, bullying, intimidating. You wanted to know who she'd told, but she'd never told anyone except Harrison. Then you screwed up. You took her from me, and you shouldn't have done that."

Henry stiffened his limbs and released a scream that seemed to come all the way from his toes.

Christopher's eyes flashed hot. The hard set of his lips and rigidity of his stance warned her to tread carefully, but Emma stormed ahead.

"You're going to jail," she said, bouncing Henry gently in her arms. "It's only a matter of time now."

He shot Sara a fevered look, then fisted his hands

into his messy hair. "You," he seethed, glaring at the woman he'd clearly abused for a week.

"You," she yelled back, angry and suddenly looking utterly unafraid. "You stole hundreds of thousands of dollars from local families who were already struggling to pay their bills and buy groceries. You helped yourself to a portion of the interest they'd earned. You've killed to keep it. To cover your tracks. You're a criminal. A monster and a thief."

Christopher narrowed his eyes. "And you made me a killer."

"Greed made you a killer!"

He tipped his head back and laughed. "Now, we're going to play a game," he said, turning his attention back to Emma. "I'd originally hoped that with enough persuasion, Sara would tell me where she put the files and evidence she's collected against me, but she hasn't been very accommodating. I tried hurting her. That didn't work. I tried isolating her. That didn't work. Food deprivation didn't work. Now the police have one of my men in custody, and he's sure to squeal on me to save his idiot brothers, so I need to get out of town fast. I can't go without those files. I didn't work this hard to become a fugitive living on the run."

"What kind of game?" Emma asked, circling back to what mattered and not caring if Christopher had to live in a cave in Tombouctou.

He fixed her with a warning stare, then sidestepped until he had a clear view of Sara on the floor behind her. "The game goes like this—Sara either tells me where the evidence is, or Sara watches while her baby sister and tiny nephew die slow, ugly deaths."

Emma moved back another step, putting more space between Henry and Christopher. "What about the Finn boys?" she asked. "You said you're in a hurry because they're going to turn on you. Will you kill them too? All of them?" She wrinkled her nose in challenge. "Seems like you might get one or two, but whoever's left will either get the best of you or get away and turn you in."

"You're forgetting that accidents happen, and those guys go everywhere together," Christopher said.

"Another case of cut brake lines?" she asked. Emma struggled not to be sick. He spoke about killing three brothers as coolly as if he were talking about the weather.

The building sound of an ATV engine turned Christopher to the door. "Excellent. He's here." He clapped his palms together. "That game we talked about starts now. You have three minutes to give me what I want or choose who dies first."

"You'll kill us all anyway," Sara said. "Why would I give you anything?"

Christopher smiled and pressed the door wide. "Three minutes," he said, shooting his gun into the air for emphasis before letting the barrier slam shut behind him.

SAWYER HAD LOST count of the number of acres he'd covered when he heard the gunshot. He'd been at it for hours and not found any trace of Sara or anyone else, and at just before dawn, the single gunshot seemed all kinds of wrong.

He'd left Emma and Henry inside a heavily secured home, protected by a state-of-the-art system, but instinct had his hand inside his pocket, seeking his cell phone anyway.

He frowned at the pitiful single bar of service, then dialed Emma, thankful to have any reception so deep in the forest. No answer.

He redialed and squinted at the slowly lightening sky while he waited. The sun would rise soon, and he'd be able to see farther, move faster, finish his mission and return to his family. That was how he thought of them now, he realized. *As his family.* His new team.

He dialed again, and the call went to voice mail. Sawyer's intuition flared. He dialed the number of the officer posted outside his home instead.

That call went to voice mail, as well.

Sawyer broke into a sprint, running full speed in the direction of his vehicle. This time, he dialed Detective Miller.

"This is Sawyer Lance," he stated without waiting for the customary hello when the call connected. "Have you heard from your man outside my home?"

"No," Miller answered hesitantly. "Where are you?"

"Looking for Sara, but Emma's not answering, and

neither is her security patrol. I've just heard a gunshot. I think someone's taken her and Henry like they took Sara, and I think they're somewhere on Finn land with her now."

"Whoa," Detective Miller cautioned. "Slow down and start over. Where are you?" he asked again.

"Detective," Sawyer said through gritted teeth, feeling his temper flare, "check on my family. Call me when it's done. I'll fill you in after." He disconnected. His mind spun with calculations as he ran. The amount of time it would take him to return home. The amount of time it would take him to reach the Finns' home. The amount of time it would take to find the location of the gunshot based on the echo and his best guess.

His phone vibrated in his palm as he slid behind the wheel of his rented SUV. "Lance," he answered.

There was a long beat of silence before the detective spoke. "Emma made a 911 call late last night, when responders arrived, the home was empty. Your bedroom window was broken. Our man was down."

Sawyer beat his empty palm against the steering wheel and floored the gas pedal. He reversed down the long dirt road at the edge of the Finn property with abandon. Dirt flew in a cloud around him. "They were home when I left," Sawyer said. "I have the car, so where the hell are they?" He thought for a moment about the situation. "Did you say she called 911?" He pulled the phone away to check the screen. He'd missed four calls. Two from a number he recognized as belonging to the new security system. Two from Detective Miller. His teeth gnashed as he swung the vehicle around at the end of the lane. "You called," he said. "It never rang." Cell service wasn't any good on the mountain. Nothing but trees and wildlife for miles. No signs of civilization.

Sawyer swallowed past a growing lump in his throat as numerous horrific images cluttered his mind. "Were there signs of a struggle?" he asked, unable to bring himself to ask the bigger question. Was there blood?

"Just the broken window," Miller said. "Someone shut off the alarm using the code, but no one answered when the contact number was called."

"It didn't ring," Sawyer said. He spun the SUV at the end of the lane and shifted hard into Drive. There wasn't anything to be done at his place. Emma and Henry were already gone. The cops would slow him down with questions for their reports, and time was already wasting. He needed a new plan. "I'm going to the Finn house."

"You are not," Detective Miller ordered, his voice thick with authority.

"I am," Sawyer corrected. "If you don't want me there, I suggest you try to stop me."

A siren coughed to life on the other end of the line. Challenge accepted. "You've got no business—" Miller began.

Sawyer cut him off. Miller didn't get to decide what was or was not Sawyer's business, and Emma and Henry absolutely were. "I've been on the Finn property all night," Sawyer interjected. "Walking. Looking."

"Trespassing," Miller countered, the siren on his vehicle complaining in the background.

"Looking for places Sara might've been held. I didn't hurt anything. Didn't touch anything."

"Did you find anything?"

"No, but there's a lot more ground to cover, and I heard a gunshot. It was near, but not near enough that I could say where it came from specifically, and I don't have time to mess around trying not to infringe on other folks' rights when my rights and the rights of my family have been trodden over daily for a week. So, like I said, I'm going to talk to the Finns. If you don't want me there or you're just eager to charge me with trespassing, then you'd better come haul me in." He disconnected and dropped the phone onto his passenger seat, then depressed the gas pedal and tore up the quiet country road getting to the Finns' house.

He took his time pulling into the driveway, careful not to roll into an ambush. He parked several yards from the front porch and climbed out as the sun crested the horizon. Senses on alert, and one hand on the butt of his gun, Sawyer opened the driver's door.

The home's front door swung open a moment later. A man in bib-style Carhartt overalls walked out. His clothes were covered in old grease stains. His boots and ball cap looked equally well-worn. "Who's there?" he called, stepping onto the top porch step.

Sawyer remained partially behind the open door. "Sawyer Lance, Fortress Security," he announced. "I'm hoping you have a minute to talk."

"I have a minute," he said, "but the missus is making breakfast, and I try not to miss a meal. Can I ask what this is about?" Mr. Finn was pushing fifty, tall and lean with a mess of crow's-feet at the corner of each eye.

"Are you Mr. Finn?" Sawyer asked.

"That's right. I'm Mark Finn." He hooked his thumbs in the straps of his bibs, both hands visible.

Sawyer relaxed and shut the car door. "Mr. Finn, I'm here because my…" He paused, stuck for the word. His *what*? His girlfriend? The term felt far too juvenile for what Emma was to him. She was everything to him. She and Henry. He rolled his shoulders and began again, reminding himself that time was speeding ahead while he floundered in a stranger's driveway, worried about semantics and courtesies. "My baby and his mama were abducted last night, and there was a gunshot out this way not long ago. I'm worried she might be on your property somewhere and hurt." *Or worse*, he thought. But there had only been one gunshot. There were two of them. A mama and a son.

"I heard that shot," Mr. Finn said, trading his easy smile for a frown. "Could be anything. Everyone's got a rifle out here. Could be someone saw a snake. Maybe had target practice or whatnot."

"No," Sawyer interrupted. "It wasn't target practice. There was only one shot, Mr. Finn." He felt the tension in the air, saw the man's shoulders square, his chin rise. "I'm not here to accuse you of anything. I'm looking for your help."

Mr. Finn crossed his arms and whistled. "I think you should go."

A moment later a dog the size of Texas tore into view, shaggy, caked in mud and rocketing to a seat at Finn's side.

Sawyer divided his attention, wishing he'd left the door open between himself and the massive mutt. "One of your sons was arrested last night," Sawyer said flatly. "I know because he and his crew came into my home in search of my family. I held them off. Shot one. The others got away clean. David was arrested. I think the others came back while I was out today, and I'm afraid that shot was meant for either my baby or his mama "

Mr. Finn's face went pale. "My boys wouldn't do anything like that. You're mistaken and out of line for coming here like this, and you'd do best to go."

"No, sir," Sawyer said. "I can't do that. See, I need you to tell me where a woman could be held on your property without being noticed for a week. Maybe two women now and my baby. Then I want to look for them."

Mr. Finn's sheet-white skin paled further, leaning on a shade of green. "No."

The half bark of a police siren shut Sawyer's mouth, already open for a rebuttal.

Behind him, Detective Miller bounced his black truck over the pitted gravel drive, bubble light flashing on top of his vehicle.

The door to the home opened again. This time a woman in jeans and a button-down rushed out. She had silver in her dark ponytail and a kid on one hip. A boy half her height trailed after her. "What's this about, Mark?" she called. "I'm just about to serve breakfast."

Mark let his eyes shut slowly, then turned to repeat Sawyer's story with a gentler touch than Sawyer had delivered it.

Detective Miller slammed his truck door, then hastened up the drive to where they stood. He pressed his palms to his hips and glared at Sawyer. "Have you said your piece?"

Sawyer nodded. "I have."

"Good. Like I told you before, we can't legally access their land without a warrant. So, you need to leave or be arrested for trespassing."

"I'm not leaving," Sawyer said. He turned desperate, pleading eyes on Mrs. Finn. "Please, ma'am," he pressed. "My four-month-old son and his mama are missing. I believe they're both in grave danger, and I think someone is holding them on your property. All I want is the chance to look for them. If they're not here, I'll leave, apologize, refine my search. But I'm asking you—what would you do if you thought your spouse and one of your babies was being held

on my property? What if I said you weren't allowed
to look for them?"

Mrs. Finn shifted the kid on her hip and traded
a look with her husband. She turned a serious gaze
on Sawyer. "You got something of theirs with you?"

Sawyer scrambled to make sense of the question.
"What?"

"A shirt, a blanket, a hair tie," she said. "It don't
matter." She tucked her fingers in her mouth and
whistled. A mess of kids came running. "These ain't
all ours, but they'll help if they want breakfast, and
you know they do. Blue will help too, if you've got
something he can use to track." She nodded at the
dog.

"Yes." Sawyer spun around, wrenching the SUV
door open and digging behind the seats for something belonging to Emma or Henry. "Thank you," he
said, fighting a punch of emotion. He came up with
a blue blanket of Henry's and a hoodie of Emma's.

Blue gave the items a long sniff, then took off in
search of more of those same scents.

The Finns, Detective Miller and a slew of kids
from age five to fifteen fanned out across the back-
yard, headed into the woods.

"We've got a number of barns and outbuildings,"
Mr. Finn said as they crossed the wide, flat space
behind the house. "The kids and I have built blinds,
forts, tree houses, all that and more on this land over
the years." He slowed as his family and neighbor kids

slipped out of sight, no more than silhouettes against a brilliant morning sky.

Sawyer ached to run after Blue, who was long gone, but waited, anticipated what Mr. Finn had to say. The way he'd paled at the mention of his other sons had meant something. Sawyer hoped it meant he had a good idea where Emma and Henry might be.

Finn swung a worried gaze from Sawyer to Detective Miller and halted in his tracks.

Miller cocked a hip. "You got something on your mind, Mark?"

Mr. Finn scanned the trees. "When my oldest boy was in high school, he'd throw wild parties at a spot we call The Point. It's just a small plot of flat land where my great-granddad's house stood about a hundred and fifty years back, but the last time I was out that way, there was a shed still standing." He pointed in the direction opposite of where the others had gone. "There's an access road a couple miles from here that cuts back this way. Down near Pine Creek Road."

"I know it," Detective Miller said, pulling keys from his pocket. "I drove past it getting here." He smiled at Sawyer. "I can be there in about ten minutes. You coming, Lance?"

"No." Sawyer shook Finn's hand with gusto, then broke into a sprint. "I can be there in seven."

Chapter Eighteen

"Go!" Sara whispered frantically to Emma. "Please." She struggled to hold back the silent sobs racking her battered body.

Emma fought the urge to lose control right along with her sister, but that was a luxury Emma didn't have. She was unharmed and unbound. It was up to her to get them all out of there. Alive.

Henry squirmed in her arms. He'd screamed himself to sleep during the argument with Christopher, but he was restless. Ready to wake. To scream again. Ready for a bottle. A new diaper. All the things Emma couldn't provide for him.

"Go," Sara continued.

"No." Emma tilted forward, locking determined eyes on her sister. "I'm not leaving you here to be murdered."

"Think of Henry," Sara sobbed. "If you're still here when that door opens again, someone's going to die."

"He's going to kill us all regardless," Emma said.

"The minute you tell him what he wants to know, you'll no longer be useful and we'll no longer have leverage. We'll all be dead the next second. So pull it together and help me think."

"You have to try to get away," Sara begged. "You have no idea what he's capable of." Tears rolled over her bruised cheeks, through the squint of her swollen black eye. She pulled her knees to her chest, and the ideas of what Sara might have been through came at Emma like a tidal wave.

"If he comes back and we're gone, he'll kill you," Emma explained. "Henry will hear the shot and scream, giving away our position, then Christopher will kill us. That's if Henry doesn't start crying the minute I lay him down to slide through the hole. Once I get out—if I get out—I can't even hide in the shadows anymore. The sun is up."

Sara pulled in a sharp breath; her cries quieted. She blinked at the warm rays of orange and amber light cutting through the shed's ceiling. "Another day," she said, mesmerized. "Every night I think I won't see another day."

Emma paced the small room with Henry in her good arm, forcing her thoughts away from the pain of her broken wrist. Outside, the sound of an approaching engine grew louder, closer, before the silence. "We need a plan, or you're right—there won't be another day. Not for any of us."

"Maybe we can hold the door shut somehow," Sara suggested.

Emma shook her head. "If we try to stop him from coming in, he'll just shoot through the door and hit us both. Besides, I can hear a second voice. There are two men now, and we aren't stronger than two men. I think my wrist is broken, and you look like you haven't eaten in a week."

"I've tried," Sara whispered. "When they bring it, I try."

Emma leaned her forehead to the wall and angled for a look at the new arrival between cracks in the rickety wooden boards.

"Who is it?" Sara asked.

"I think it's one of the Finn boys," she said. Though she hadn't gotten a clear look at him in the dark, she thought he might have been one of the two men on the dock while she'd hidden in the water. If she was right, then he'd already come to abduct and kill her once. Considering that she was currently abducted, it was an easy jump to the reason he was there now.

The newcomer climbed off his ATV with a gun on his hip. His shaggy red hair was unkempt, and his eyes were wild. His gaze jumped from the shed to Christopher. "I was thinking," he said nervously. "I think we can get this done another way. There's no one at either house now. We can leave them here, and while everyone's out hunting for them, we can go through both places, take another look. Find what we missed."

"No time," Christopher said. "I need to go, which

means they need to go. You got that? If I come back here on my way out of town and find any of them alive, I'm coming for your family. All of them. Maybe I'll build a nice middle-of-the-night fire to take care of all those young siblings. Maybe a brutal car accident for your woman and your baby. While you're grieving over their twisted carnage, you'll know it was your fault. All because you couldn't do this one simple task. You want that?"

"No, man," Finn said. "I didn't want anyone to die." He scraped a heavy hand over his cheek. "I never agreed to this. You never said anything about kidnapping and murder."

"I just did." Christopher climbed onto his vehicle and started the engine. "I've got to get this ride scrubbed down in case her or that kid drooled on it. They'll check it for DNA when they find it, and I don't need any other fingers pointed my way. I gave Sara three minutes to tell you where she hid the evidence. If she doesn't, then you've got to make her choose who to shoot first. Don't make me a liar."

"What if she tells me what you want to know?"

Christopher drew a finger across his neck. "Kill them anyway. No loose ends. Understand?"

"What about the baby?" Finn asked. "You said I could take it to a fire station. Give it a chance at a life."

"I'm going home to pack," Christopher said, ignoring Finn's question. "There's a hole in the back wall big enough for them to fit through. If you take too long going in, they'll force you to chase them. It's awful damn early for that, trust me." He stuffed the helmet onto his head and flipped the visor up. "I want to see three bodies when I come back, so do. Your. Job." He delivered the final three words with deliberate menace, then revved his engine to life.

Emma's heart leaped and twisted in her throat. "Sit up," she told Sara. "Scoot back, sit up. Hurry."

Sara obeyed. Bending her knees, she planted her bound feet on the floor and pressed her back to the wall, settling her bound wrists in front of her.

Emma set Henry on Sara's lap, fitting him into the sharp curve of her sister's body for balance, then she dragged them both against the wall beside the door.

Next, Emma ran for the hole. "Don't let him fall."

Sara gripped Henry's legs in her hands. "What are you doing?" Sara gasped. "You can't leave him with me. I can't protect him."

"I'm not leaving," Emma said, crouching to grab the edge of a broken board in her good hand. She braced her feet against the floor and leaned back, throwing her weight into the movement, arm straining, legs burning. "Come on," she whispered. Nothing happened.

She inched forward, rearranged her grip on the wood and tried again.

"What are you doing?" Sara repeated. "Get out and take Henry."

"I'm not leaving. I've only got one arm to hold Henry while I run through the forest in broad daylight with him screaming. We'll be dead inside five minutes." Her grip slid. She reset her efforts and tried again. "He'll give chase. He'll hunt us."

The board made a moaning creak.

"So what?" Sara asked. "You have to try. Why are you making the hole bigger if not to run?"

The board gave way with a sudden, shockingly loud crack, showering the floor in shards of rotted wood and sending Emma onto her backside with a thump. A smile broke over her lips. "I can't run, but I can fight."

Outside, a man swore, and the door rattled.

Emma grabbed her newly freed slat of weak, aged wood and ran to hide beside the door with Sara and Henry. And wait.

SAWYER'S CHEST THROBBED with the effort of an all-out run up an uneven, rocky grade toward the mountaintop where Mark Finn had suggested Emma and Henry might be held. Maybe Sara too. His leg muscles burned. His worried heart hammered from effort and fear. It had been too long since he'd heard that single gunshot. *A kill shot*, he thought. And even if she hadn't died immediately, she'd have bled out by now, with all the time he'd wasted asking Finn's permission to look. Then again, without Finn's input, he would have had no idea where to go. Now he knew there was a shed, and Emma might be there with Henry. The thought pushed him harder, faster.

Maybe Emma had gotten away. Maybe the shot had missed her, and she'd hidden.

Maybe she had made the shot.

Sawyer slowed at the low groan of an ATV and walked silently in the sound's direction. Through the dense growth of ancient trees, a black ATV rumbled downhill with only a driver on board.

EMMA WIDENED HER STANCE, raised the board onto her shoulder like a baseball bat and waited as the door wiggled, then opened.

And she swung.

The wood connected with the man's face in a gush of blood and curses. Her weapon split down the center in response, one long ragged crack, splinters of rot flying over the both of them. He stumbled back, blood pouring from his nose and mouth, eyes blinking, ready to fall. The man's arms flailed, hands reached out for balance and caught the doorjamb with a thud.

The gun in his hand went off.

Sara screamed. Emma gasped.

Searing pain scorched through Emma's side and her hand lowered to the spot on instinct. Her palm slid against a strange, slick warmth, and the world tilted, but the man didn't fall.

Not good.

She needed to knock him out, steal his ATV and race her son and sister to safety.

"You shot her!" Sara screamed. "Emma!"

Emma looked at her side, then her palms, confused and swimming in adrenaline. Blood seeped through her shirt. The eye-crossing, relentless pain came next. She locked her teeth and swung the wood again, heart in her mouth, pulse beating like thunder through her head.

This time, the man's hand shot out and caught the busted board. He wrenched it from her grip and threw it out the door behind him. "You broke my nose!" he wailed. Blood trailed over his lips, teeth and chin. The skin along the ridge of his nose was red, broken and quickly swelling. His eyes flamed hot.

Emma stumbled back, pressing both palms to her side, where blood flowed freely around and between her fingers now. Her broken wrist no longer ached, but her knees wobbled. Her head spun, and the pain of the gunshot chewed its way straight through her. The unconscionable burn radiated across her gut and up her chest until it ate through her vision, and the filthy, aged floorboards rushed up to meet her.

A SECOND GUNSHOT. Sawyer pulled his phone and his gun, double-timing his pace up the mountain toward the peak, where he hoped to find a shed, and Emma, Henry and Sara alive.

"Miller," the detective answered.

"Another shot," Sawyer said flatly, forcing his mind and body to stay tuned to the task. "Hear it?"

"I heard it. Got an ambulance coming."

Sawyer's shoulders relaxed by a fraction. "Did you get the ATV?"

"Yes, I did. Stopped him at the crossroad. Says he didn't see the no-trespassing signs and was just out for a morning drive."

Sawyer cursed. Rage burst through him like shrapnel. "You let him go?"

"No," Miller said. "He was trespassing, carrying a concealed weapon without a license, and his vehicle fits the description of an ATV seen leaving the site of multiple recent crimes. My deputy is on his way to pick him up."

"Who is he?" Sawyer fumed. "A Finn boy?"

"No. ID says Christopher Lawson."

Lawson. "He was at the credit union, standing in for the dead manager on the day that guy was murdered." Sawyer pushed himself harder, faster, his breaths coming quick and a smile forming on his lips. "I think you've gone and captured the ringleader. Don't let that one go."

"No intent of the sort," Miller said in an easy, casual drawl.

Hope rose in his chest as the next plateau came into view, and the cries of his son rose on the wind. "I've got eyes on the shed. I can hear my son crying." And there was another shiny black ATV sitting out front. If the victim of that last gunshot wasn't the driver of this ATV, then he was likely to be the next one shot. "You'd better order up another ambulance."

THE SOUNDS OF Henry's and Sara's cries warbled through Emma's fuzzy head, and she pushed to her hands and knees on autopilot. "You don't have to do this," she said, adding immediately to the pleas of her sister.

The gun shook in Finn's hand. His gaze darted around the dank, rotten, earth-scented shed. He muttered behind the other palm, which he'd clamped to his mouth.

Emma forced herself back on her haunches, deliberating, watching Finn and gauging what he might do next. Desperation drove people to do awful things, and Finn seemed as desperate as any man Emma had ever seen. "Please," she tried again. "I'm already shot, but you can save my baby and my sister. Get them away from here and tell Christopher you buried their bodies or threw them in the river. Anything. Not this for them." She lifted a bloodied palm. Fresh crimson drops painted a thick path down her forearm. "They're all the family I've got."

His face contorted with indecision. He looked at his gun, at Sara and Henry on the floor, at Emma, bleeding and weak.

"You would want to protect your family if you could, wouldn't you?" Emma asked softly, hoping that big family of his had taught him to respect and honor a genetic bond.

Finn swung in her direction, a belligerent look on his youthful face. "I have family too. He'll kill them if I don't kill you."

"He's going to kill you anyway," Emma said. "He's going to kill all of us so he can keep his stolen money and his secret, but you don't have to do this. I can see this isn't who you are, and it's not what you want." She hoped she was right.

"This was supposed to be easy money," he said. "My lady just had another baby, and we don't have money for food or diapers. My folks can't help. They're strapped raising my brothers and sisters. I can't find work without leaving town. I can't look outside town for work without a car. Can't buy a car without money." He raised his hands and pressed them to his head, pointing the gun at the ceiling. "I was going to be the muscle. A bodyguard for Christopher, a lookout when he needed me. I was going to earn enough to keep food, formula and diapers in the house until I got real work. Then he got his hands on my younger brothers, promising them everything. Buying them fancy ATVs and riding gear. He reeled them in and had them doing his dirty work before I even knew it was happening. Then he used them as leverage with me. If I walked out on him, he'd turn them in for the crimes he had them commit. The next thing I know, we're all doing terrible things and we're stuck."

"Now your brother David has been arrested," Emma said. "Christopher thinks he'll turn on him to keep you out of jail, so Christopher plans to kill you after you kill us."

Finn didn't blink. It was the second time she'd

told him Christopher's plans, and the second time he'd taken the information in stride.

"You already know," Emma said, letting the truth settle in. "You know, but you're still willing to become a murderer for him. Why?"

Finn paced. "It buys me and my family time."

"No, it doesn't," Emma said. "And you can't take your whole family on the run with you. Your girl and your kids, maybe, but what about your folks and all those siblings? Have you made enough money from Christopher to relocate all of them? To keep running if he looks for you?"

"He won't look for us," Finn said. "He'll be busy running from the law too."

"And if he gets caught? Turns you in to make a deal for himself?"

Finn's breaths came more quickly. A line of sweat raised on his forehead and lip. He pressed his palms to his temples. "Shut up so I can think."

Henry's cries grew desperate again, as if he was in pain. Hunger, Emma thought. When was the last time he'd eaten? Before bed last night. It was also the last time he'd been changed. Tears pricked her eyes. Her baby was hungry, and she couldn't feed him. Scared and she couldn't hold him.

Finn dropped his hands and looked from Emma to Sara. "Enough. Turn around. Both of you." He pressed his thumb to the hammer on his gun and pulled it back with a soft click that rolled Emma's stomach. "I just want this to be over," he said, exhausted. "Turn around. I'll make it quick. Three shots. Three seconds. You'll never know it happened, and it'll be over."

"Please," Sara cried. "Don't."

Finn scooped Henry into his arms and set him against the wall, near the hole Emma had made. He dragged Sara back against the far wall, opposite the door, and he motioned Emma into the space between her son and sister. Lining them up like bottles for target practice. "Close your eyes."

Emma gripped her side and reached for her baby. Finn groaned, "Stop."

Emma couldn't stop. It wasn't in her. Henry was alone, crying, scared. He wouldn't die alone like that. She didn't care what Finn or anyone else said. "Mama's here," she called, working her voice into something less soaked in pain, less mired in grief. "Shh," she cooed.

"I said stop!" Finn raged, his boot connecting with her torso, spinning her into a hard roll that ended with a collision against the side wall, away from Henry and the escape hole. The impact stole her breath, knocked the wind from her lungs. She searched wildly through spotted vision for Henry when she stilled.

"Henry," she choked.

His cries were there, but he wasn't. Her gaze darted across the floor. Had he flailed and kicked himself through the hole? Had he fallen to the ground?

Emma's heart and stomach lurched.

Finn stormed forward, peering through the hole. "What the...?" He stood upright as Henry's cries grew distant and muffled. Panic colored his bloody face. "I should've just killed you all the minute I walked in here," he said, storming for the door. "I let you talk to me and get into my head, now..."

A blast of gunfire cut Finn's rant short. The sudden burst rang in Emma's ears and vibrated in her chest. Finn flew backward, arms waving, feet twisting, until he landed in a lifeless heap beside Sara.

The door swung open and Sara screamed.

A pair of men marched inside.

Emma's mind reeled. What had happened? Who had arrived? Who had shot Finn? Christopher?

The first man kicked the gun away from Finn, then lowered to check his neck for a pulse.

"Emma." Sawyer's voice broke through her muddled thoughts. His face swam into view, marred with fear and concern. He crouched before her, Henry crying in his arms. He pressed his forehead to hers, then kissed her lips with firm reassurance. "Sorry I'm late."

Detective Miller stood, stepped away from Finn's body. "He's gone," he said sadly, then moved to Sara's side and cut easily through her ropes with a pocketknife. Once she was freed, he hoisted her into his arms and carried her straight outside and into the day.

Sawyer's expression fell. His eyes stretched wide as he lifted a bloodied palm between them. "Emma?"

His gaze trailed over her torso, over the smears of her blood on Henry's pajamas between them. "You've been shot."

Emma opened her mouth to tell him she was okay, that she loved him, but the words didn't come. She felt the strength of his arms around her. Smelled the sweet scent of Henry's baby shampoo as her head rolled back. Her thoughts fell into darkness.

Chapter Nineteen

Sawyer kissed Emma lightly under the canopy of lights outside her home. A lot had changed in the eight months since he'd ridden with her, breathless and terrified, to the hospital following her mountain-top rescue. His pulse still raced whenever he thought of that day. He still dreamed every manner of horrific scenarios where things went another way. Sometimes he arrived five minutes later. Too late to save her. He hated those dreams most. But when the nightmares of losing her woke him now, the way nightmares of losing his team had woken him before, he simply reached for her in the darkness and pulled her near. Then everything was right in the world.

"I love you," she whispered against his crisp white dress shirt, playfully flipping the end of his tie.

He kissed her again, at a complete loss for words.

Seeing her so healthy and beautiful under the end-less rows of twinkle lights, surrounded by family and friends, it was hard to believe that he'd nearly lost her completely. She'd gone limp in his arms, and he'd felt the punch of it in his gut as clear and strong as if it would kill him too.

Eight months since he'd stood sentinel at her bedside following her surgery. Eight months since he'd prayed around the clock to see her beautiful blue eyes once more. Eight months since he'd fallen to his knees the moment she'd spoken his name and begged her to be his wife. He hadn't gotten halfway through the rambling proposal before she'd said yes. It was her first word after three long days of silence, and it had the power to change his life.

She cradled his cheek in her palm as she smiled.

Two hundred guests and she only had eyes for him. His chest puffed in pride and satisfaction.

"What?" she asked.

"Just thinking about how lucky I am. How thankful," he said. It was a reminder he gave her often. "The hospital staff wasn't sure you'd make it." They'd said she lost a lot of blood on that mountain, too much for good odds.

"But you knew I would," she said.

"Yes, I did," he agreed. "They didn't know you like I do." They didn't know what Emma would do, what she'd endure or survive for the chance to raise her son.

Sawyer knew, and he'd waited patiently at her bedside with Henry and Sara until one day, Emma simply opened her eyes.

"Well, that makes us two lucky, thankful people," she said, sliding her palms gently against his chest.

Sawyer lifted her left hand and kissed the knuckles beside her engagement ring. The ring had been her mother's, but Sara had insisted Emma wear it after the engagement. Sawyer had a custom wedding band in the works to go with her mother's ring. She'd wear that soon too. For now, they'd settled on an open house–style engagement party where friends, families and neighbors could get a look at the girls they'd read about in newspapers and gossip columns straight through Christmas. The community had followed Emma's and Sara's recoveries like their own lives depended on it.

"Enough of that," a familiar voice boomed nearby. Detective Miller approached with Sara on his arm. Their flirting had started at the hospital, both checking in on Emma, and it continued to the present. Sawyer thought it was nice. Emma was more cautious, expectedly protective of her big sister, despite the fact that, to Sawyer's opinion, Miller had been a perfect gentleman every step of the way. "Save it for the ceremony," Miller said with a broad grin.

Sawyer gave Miller's hand a hearty shake. He owed the detective more than he could ever repay. Thanks to his dogged follow-up work, Christopher Lawson was in jail and going to stay there for a very long time. The expected charges of murder, attempted murder, embezzlement, kidnapping and a half dozen of others were just the tip of the iceberg once Miller got started. He'd combed through Christopher's personal computer as if it held the secrets of the universe, and he'd uncovered a treasure trove of evidence against Christopher in the process. Miller linked him and his accomplices to a bevy of other criminal offenses within the month. As a bonus, and as no surprise to the detective, David Finn had confessed everything he knew in trade for leniency on his brothers. Christopher turned on everyone in the hopes of reducing his sentence, but the FBI had been particularly interested in the money laundering and fraud. And they weren't interested in giving breaks.

Sawyer released his hand. "Sorry, man, I just can't seem to keep my hands off of her."

"So I've heard" was Miller's quick response. It earned him an elbow from Sara and a grin from Emma.

She pulled Sara into a hug. "Thank you for doing all this," she said. "Everything is absolutely beautiful, completely over-the-top for an engagement party."

Sara stroked Emma's arm as she stepped back. "Consider this a test run for the big day."

Emma smiled into the apricot-hued horizon, lifting her chin to the warm setting sun. "I still can't believe I'm getting married on our land. Just like Mom and Dad."

"They'd be really happy," Sara said, tearing up. "I'm still just really glad you're alive."

Sawyer worked to swallow the brick of emotion that presented at the slightest reminder.

"Back at ya," Emma said.

Thankfully, Emma's broken wrist had healed as nicely as her gunshot wound. Both under constant watch and care from Sawyer and Sara, not to mention an endless string of casseroles and pies hand delivered by community members, a testimony and staple of courtesy in the South.

Sara leaned against her new beau's side, her gaze floating across the sea of people on her lawn. "I'd started thinking of Emma and I as alone in the world after Mom and Dad died, but there are nearly two hundred people here tonight, and we're expecting a hundred more for the wedding in September." She eyeballed Sawyer. "Though I think half these guests belong to you."

He smiled. "Probably so." The group near the stables, for example, now roaring with laughter as Henry toddled after a barn cat. He recognized every face from his team at Fortress Security, plus Wyatt's new wife and baby. The rest of that crowd was blood-related and soon to be Emma and Sara's family, as well. Most of them were Garretts. Cousins from Kentucky that seemed to have *protect and serve* in their blood.

For a pair of sisters so accustomed to being alone, Emma and Sara were in for a major adjustment. Henry would never know a day without someone to play with.

Sawyer's partner, Wyatt, caught him staring and led half the pack in Sawyer's direction. Wyatt's new wife laughed along behind them, leading Henry by one hand. His cousins' wives herded everyone else in his direction.

"Well, here comes a crowd," Sawyer muttered to his little circle, a smile already spreading on his lips. "What do you suppose they're up to?"

Wyatt pulled Sawyer in for a strong one-armed hug, then kissed Emma's and Sara's cheeks and shook Miller's hand. "We were just talking about the happy couple," he said, looking from Emma to Sawyer, then back.

Sawyer's senses went on alert. "What are you up to?"

Others from the lawn began a sweep in their direction, whispering and pointing as they moved.

Wyatt pressed a palm to his heart, feigning innocence. Poorly. "Henry was just telling us the story of how two quiet sisters single-handedly took down a psychopathic murderer, escaped abduction and ended a mass of fraud and embezzlement operations, armed only with wood from the dilapidated shed where they were held."

Emma laughed as Henry made a stumbling run for her calves. "Is that right?" she asked. "I know his vocabulary is up to fifteen words now, but I'm not sure he's mastered *dilapidated* or *psychopathic murderer* just yet."

"You'd be surprised," Wyatt said.

Sawyer hoisted Henry into his arms, awed as usual by the sensation of looking into a mirror or at a living photo from his youth. He kissed his son and felt the familiar tug of pride.

"What are you thinking?" Emma asked, smiling again, her skin aglow in the slowly setting sun.

"I'm just all kinds of happy," he said.

Emma beamed, all eyes on her as the crowd grew silent. "Well, I'm glad," she said, digging into the pocket of her pale pink sundress. "Because I have an early wedding present for you." She opened her palm to him, revealing a small scroll in the center. The little paper was tied with two thin white ribbons.

Sawyer dipped his head, unsure. "Is this a bride thing?" he asked, taking the scroll between his thumb and first finger for examination.

Emma smiled. "Open it."

He frowned, especially cautious with any surprise that his entire family and group of friends seemed to be in on. "You said it's a wedding gift?" he asked, removing and pocketing the white ribbons, then unfurling the white paper with his thumbs while Henry did his best to grab it from him.

"More like—" Emma paused and grinned impossibly wider "—Christmas gifts."

"Christmas gifts? It's the middle of summer." Sawyer made a sour face and kept unrolling. That clue didn't help him at all. Finally, he turned the paper over in his fingers. One heavy black square occupied the center of the slick white paper. A grayish semicircle centered in that. In the semicircle were two white peanut shapes. Some sparse text rode along the top. The date. *Yesterday.* His last name. *Lance.* The name of the hospital where Emma had been treated last fall. *Mercy General Hospital.* The word *female.* Written twice. "What is this?" He lifted his eyes to the group, who looked collectively disappointed in him.

He knew what he thought it was, but he didn't dare jump to conclusions that might bring him unnecessarily to tears in front of two hundred people.

"Here." Emma slid in close and pulled Henry onto her hip. She pointed to the first peanut. "This is your daughter." She slid her finger to the next peanut. "And this is also your daughter." She stepped back and watched him, one hand set protectively on her stomach.

"What?" He'd been right? Babies? He stared at the little paper through quickly blurring eyes. "You're really pregnant?"

She nodded, eyes glistening. "That's right, Sawyer Lance," she said. "In a few weeks, we'll marry and become an official family of three. But by the end of the year we'll be a family of five."

"Pregnant," Sawyer's gaze slid to her middle. He'd missed all this the first time. He'd longed for an opportunity to see her glow and bloom again one day. A day when he could be there for her. For anything she needed. That day was already here.

"Yes." She smiled.

"Twins?"

"Girls," she answered.

And like the day she'd opened her eyes in that hospital room, Sawyer knelt before her. This time, he kissed her belly through the soft fabric of her sundress, then rose to kiss her nose, her forehead, her cheeks and her mouth as the crowd burst into whoops and applause.

* * * * *

Look for more books in Julie Anne Lindsey's Fortress Security miniseries later this year.

And don't miss the previous book in the series:

Deadly Cover-Up

Available now from Harlequin Intrigue!

SPECIAL EXCERPT FROM

⊕HARLEQUIN

INTRIGUE

*Sheriff Jamison Wyatt has never forgotten Liza Dean,
the one who got away. But now she's back, and she needs
his help to find her sister. They'll have to infiltrate a crime
syndicate, but once they're on the inside, will they
be able to get back out?*

Read on for a sneak preview of
South Dakota Showdown *by Nicole Helm.*

Chapter One

Bonesteel, South Dakota, wasn't even a dot on most maps, which
was precisely why Jamison Wyatt enjoyed being its attached
officer. Though he was officially a deputy with the Valiant County
Sheriff's Department, as attached officer his patrol focused on
Bonesteel and its small number of residents.

One of six brothers, he wasn't the only Wyatt who acted as an
officer of the law—but he was the only man who'd signed up for
the job of protecting Bonesteel.

He'd grown up in the dangerous, unforgiving world of a biker
gang run by his father. The Sons of the Badlands were a cutthroat
group who'd been wreaking havoc on the small communities of
South Dakota—just like this one—for decades.

Luckily, Jamison had spent the first five years of his life on his
grandmother's ranch before his mother had fully given in to Ace
Wyatt and moved them into the fold of the nomadic biker gang.

Through tenacity and grit Jamison had held on to a belief in
right and wrong that his grandmother had instilled in him in those
early years. When his mother had given birth to son after son on the
inside of the Sons, Jamison had known he would get them out—
and he had, one by one—and escape to their grandmother's ranch
situated at the very edge of Valiant County.

HIEXP0220

It was Jamison's rough childhood in the gang and the immense responsibility he'd placed on himself to get his brothers away from it that had shaped him into a man who took everything perhaps a shade too seriously. Or so his brothers said.

Jamison had no regrets on that score. Seriousness kept people safe. He was old enough now to enjoy the relative quiet of patrolling a small town like Bonesteel. He had no desire to see lawbreaking. He'd seen enough. But he had a deep, abiding desire to make sure everything was right.

So it was odd to be faced with a clear B and E just a quarter past nine at night on the nearly deserted streets. Maybe if it had been the general store or gas station, he might have understood. But the figure was trying to break into his small office attached to city hall.

It was bold and ridiculous enough to be moderately amusing. Probably a drunk, he thought. Maybe the…woman—yes, it appeared to be a woman—was drunk and looking to sleep it off.

When he did get calls, they were often alcohol related and mostly harmless, as this appeared to be.

Since Jamison was finishing up his normal last patrol for the night, he was on foot. He walked slowly over, keeping his steps light and his body in the shadows. The streets were quiet, having long since been rolled up for the night.

Still, the woman worked on his doorknob. If she was drunk, she was awfully steady for one. Either way, she didn't look to pose much of a threat.

He stepped out of the shadow. "Typically people who break and enter are better at picking a lock."

The woman stopped what she was doing—but she hadn't jumped or shrieked or even stumbled. She just stilled.

Don't miss
South Dakota Showdown by Nicole Helm,
available March 2020 wherever
Harlequin Intrigue books and ebooks are sold.

Harlequin.com

Love Harlequin romance?

DISCOVER.

Be the first to find out about promotions,
news and exclusive content!

Facebook.com/HarlequinBooks

Twitter.com/HarlequinBooks

Instagram.com/HarlequinBooks

Pinterest.com/HarlequinBooks

ReaderService.com

EXPLORE.

Sign up for the Harlequin e-newsletter and
download a free book from any series at
TryHarlequin.com

CONNECT.

Join our Harlequin community to
share your thoughts and connect
with other romance readers!
Facebook.com/groups/HarlequinConnection